DEVIL'S DUE

Center Point
Large Print

Also by James Clay and available from
Center Point Large Print:

Songbird of the West
Gunfighter's Revenge

**This Large Print Book carries the
Seal of Approval of N.A.V.H.**

DEVIL'S DUE

James Clay

CENTER POINT LARGE PRINT
THORNDIKE, MAINE

This Center Point Large Print edition
is published in the year 2021 by arrangement with
the author.

Copyright © 2018 by James Clay.

All rights reserved.

The text of this Large Print edition is unabridged.
In other aspects, this book may vary
from the original edition.
Printed in the United States of America
on permanent paper.
Set in 16-point Times New Roman type.

ISBN: 978-1-64358-780-6

The Library of Congress has cataloged this record under
Library of Congress Control Number: 2020946341

Chapter One

Jared Ashley stepped out of the barn and felt a surge of anger, which increased as he walked toward the house. That Lilly Tantrall hadn't left yet! She was on the porch of the cabin talking with his wife. Stella's voice sounded pleasant, though she couldn't completely cover her embarrassment. "Thank you again for the clothes, Lilly. Our little girl is growing so fast right now and, well, it takes a while to get a farm to produce—"

Lilly hastily jumped in as Stella began to fumble with her words. "This is just our way of welcoming you to the West! I know how hard life out here can be. Why, when I was Becky's age, I don't think Dad had more than a dozen or so head of cattle."

Lilly Tantrall was nineteen, with long brown hair surrounding a small, pretty face highlighted by prominent cheekbones. Her short stature, a little over five feet, gave her a pixyish look. Her gracious demeanor spoke of education at a school in the East.

Jared's anger became more intense as he walked past the beautiful palomino Lilly had tethered to a post at the front of the house. His wife looked at him with pleading eyes when he stepped onto the porch. She was silently begging him not to say anything ugly.

"Jared, you remember Lilly Tantrall, you met her—"

"Yep, I met her the last time she came on one of her missions of charity."

"Jared, please—"

"If you really want to help us, Miss Tantrall, tell your father to stay away from my fences."

Lilly tried to maintain a friendly tone. "I'll tell him, Mr. Ashley. I know that sometimes cattle can knock over fences."

"It ain't the cattle that's doin' it!"

Lilly looked down briefly before smiling at Stella. "I need to be going. It was so nice seeing you again."

"Thank you, Lilly, thank you for everything."

The young woman nodded politely at Jared as she stepped off the porch. The homesteader didn't acknowledge the courtesy. He stormed inside the cabin.

"I've got the table set, Daddy." Seven-year-old Becky pointed at the dishes on the table.

"Fine," Jared's voice was toneless.

Becky didn't pick up on her father's dark mood. "How do you like my pretty new dress? Miss Lilly gave it to me today. She also gave me—"

Stella entered the cabin. She had remained outside for a few moments to calm her emotions over her husband's behaviour. "Leave your daddy alone, child. He's tired from his morning's work. Come help me get the food ready."

"Yes, Momma."

Stella Ashley's voice slashed at her husband. "Becky and I will have lunch on the table soon. Go ahead and sit down."

Jared sat down without speaking. He noticed that Becky had done a fine job of setting the table. Looking around the cabin, he once again realized how well Stella had handled her responsibilities.

It seemed that everyone was doing their job well except him.

Lunch passed with Stella giving her complete attention to their daughter. The only time her eyes went to Jared was immediately after Becky lisped through a prayer giving thanks for the food. Her glance was accusatory. Jared hadn't accompanied his wife and daughter to church for several weeks.

After the meal, Stella and Becky cleared the table. While Becky stacked the dishes and got them ready for washing, Stella took a bucket outside to the pump. Jared followed his wife and tried to speak to her as she filled the bucket with gushing water.

"I'm sorry I treated the Tantrall girl the way I did."

Stella pushed the pump handle with more force. "This was all your idea, Jared. We had a good life in Ohio. You had a decent job and we didn't have to accept charity from anyone."

"But I wasn't going anyplace at the factory. We weren't getting ahead!"

The woman let go of the pump and turned toward her husband. "Where exactly are we going now? We're one step from losing this place to the bank. You call that getting ahead!?" She picked up the bucket and returned to the house.

Jared walked back to his plowing. He wanted to tell Stella how much he loved her and Becky. He had brought them West for a better life. The homesteader laughed bitterly at his own thoughts. "Better life!" he said aloud. "We're barely surviving."

Plant and hope for a good harvest, that's all Jared knew to do. Well, maybe he should go to church with Stella and Becky and join all those folks asking the Lord for plenty of rain and no more droughts like the one last year. Couldn't hurt.

He walked around the barn to where his plow awaited him and stopped. Four men on horseback were tying ropes to his fence posts. They were going to pull down the fence with Tantrall's herd grazing less than two miles away.

"Damn Elijah Tantrall!" he whispered to himself. "The man thinks he's king, doesn't even bother to do his dirty work at night anymore."

Jared ran back to the front of the barn, grabbed

the Winchester he kept inside by the entrance and pocketed some ammunition. This time the king has made a serious mistake, Ashley thought. Tantrall would pay in blood.

Ashley ran back to his field. He was barely in range of the four intruders when he fired his first shot at them. They laughed! The invaders didn't even bother to shoot back at him. All four of them now had ropes tied to one of his fence posts. They spurred their horses at the same time and the fence came down. They laughed again, mocking how easily the fence had collapsed. They were dealing with some poor sodbuster who couldn't even put up a fence right.

Rage coursed through Jared Ashley. He ran closer to the four riders and fired again and again missed. This time one of the riders returned fire. Dust spurted near the homesteader. For the first time, he noticed that all four men had hoods over their heads.

They began to ride directly at him. Jared's rage was replaced by fear. He realized how little he had ever used a gun. There was never any need for one in Cleveland. His body trembled as he began to lever another shell into the Winchester.

Jared Ashley never got off a third shot. A bullet burrowed into his chest and he went down. All four riders stopped near the fallen homesteader. One of them dismounted, grabbed the rifle and held onto it.

"He ain't dead yet. Soon will be," the rider who had dismounted spoke. Jared heard the voice through a buzzing in his ears.

"Come on! We ain't got much time!" The second voice sounded more distant.

The thugs rode off in the direction of his cabin. Jared silently cursed himself for his stupidity. When he had spotted the outlaws, his first move should have been to protect Stella and Becky. The homesteader struggled to his feet. He staggered toward the cabin. Maybe he could still warn them.

Jared fought to maintain consciousness. He could hear loud yelps coming from the direction of his home. Smoke could suddenly be seen rising over the barn. "Stella . . . Becky . . ." Jared's voice was a raspy whisper.

The homesteader managed a few more steps. He could now hear gunshots roaring over the sounds of the fire. Screams came from both Becky and Stella. They were being brutally slaughtered.

Jared Ashley collapsed. His wife and child had been murdered. He had failed horribly: failed to protect his own family. "I'm not fit to be called a man," he whispered to the ground. Those were his last words.

Chapter Two

A procession of well-dressed men stepped silently into the Capstone Community Church. The faces on all eight men were grim. They had just returned from the cemetery and the funeral service for the Ashley family.

Seven men sat in the church's first row of pews; only one remained standing. Glenn Kagan was the head of the local Homesteaders Association. Kagan was a tall man with stooped shoulders and a large belly. Sunburns had left red blotches on his otherwise pale skin. Kagan stood at the front of the church and immediately got to the point.

"Gentlemen, yesterday an entire family was murdered in broad daylight and their home burned by a gang of vicious killers. In the past, Elijah Tantrall has been satisfied to jus' knock over fences and burn down barns. Now, he has showed what kind of man he really is: a man who will kill women and children!"

There were several murmurs of agreement. Kagan continued, "I'm demandin' that—"

The door to the church banged open and three men entered. The man leading the group was of medium height, fiftyish with hair that was still thick and still more pepper than salt. He was slim, with ropey muscles, and his body seemed to be always lurching forward as if he was looking for an opening where he could attack.

"What are you doin' here, Tantrall?!" Kagan shouted.

Tantrall laughed contemptuously. "I built this here church and it couldn't run without my money. Reckon I can walk in whenever I get the notion. Reckon I can tell men who spread lies about me to shuck off."

Kagan pointed a finger at his adversary. "I ain't lyin'!" He nodded to a young man of twenty in the first pew. "My boy Rory and I saw you—"

Tantrall's voice became a bellow. "Ya saw me knock down one of your fences, six months ago. Ya were fencin' off part of my best grazin' land." The cattle rancher pointed a thumb backward at one of the two men standing behind him. "Sheriff Thompson here told me I was breakin' the law. I paid ya for a new fence. Stop brayin' like a donkey."

Sheriff Max Thompson quickly chimed in. "Men, if any of you have somethin' that comes within shoutin' distance of proof 'bout who killed the Ashley family, or who's been pullin' down fences and burnin' barns, show it to me!"

One of the farmers, Frank Harmon, stood up slowly. He had short, thick arms and stood in a slightly bent manner from a long-ago accident.

He fidgeted with the hat in his hands as he spoke. "All of us is pretty upset right now, Sheriff. We just lost us some fine people. In the past, only property got destroyed but now it's getting down to killing. You gotta do something, Sheriff!"

The lawman stroked his thick, graying mustache. "I understand what you're sayin' but accusin' Elijah without proof is wrong. Why, on the mornin' the Ashleys was killed, Elijah's daughter took them food and clothing."

An odd silence fell over the church. Elijah Tantrall pressed his lips together and his eyes did a quick dart to the ceiling. Everyone in the room knew of Lilly Tantrall's visits to those homesteaders who were struggling the hardest but many doubted that her father approved of the charitable acts.

Sheriff Thompson shared those doubts and regretted bringing up the topic. His voice became harsh as he broke the silence. "I don't wanna hear any more fool accusations against Elijah and Lem!"

Lem Donnigan was Tantrall's foreman. He had entered the church with his boss and the sheriff. The foreman was in his mid-twenties with large muscles, calloused hands and a nose which had long ago been broken in a fight. Donnigan didn't talk much, at least not when Elijah Tantrall was around.

Tantrall stared at the farmers and spoke in

a steady voice without emotion. The rancher wasn't making a threat, he was stating a fact. "The next man who spreads lies about me will answer to me."

Elijah Tantrall turned and left. His ramrod and the sheriff followed behind him. A few minutes later, the homesteaders left the church. They had nothing more to say.

Max Thompson was grateful for the full moon, one of the few breaks he had received lately. The sheriff continued to ride the range in the vicinity of Tantrall's Circle T Ranch and the homesteaders in the dark hours. Thompson believed the daylight attack on Jared Ashley and his family had been a surprise move, something out of the ordinary. For their next brutal act the riders would likely strike, once again, at night. The sheriff knew he had to stop these raids if he wanted to prevent a land war. There had almost been an outbreak of violence that afternoon in the church,—of all places!

The lawman didn't have a dog in this fight and he could see both sides. The homesteaders were just doing what the government encouraged them to do, moving West and working the land. But men like Elijah Tantrall were a special breed. They had been here first and built ranches that had almost become empires.

Thompson stopped his horse near a section of

hills and looked upwards. What he saw reminded him of the beautiful paintings he had viewed on his last trip to Dallas. Against the backdrop of the full moon, a young woman was riding a horse toward the top of one of the hills. The horse moved swiftly and gracefully and the woman's hair swayed upward in the breeze, then playfully bounced against her shoulders.

"That could only be Lilly Tantrall," Thompson whispered to himself. "What's she doin' out at this hour of the night?"

The lawman realized it was his job to get the answer to that question. He spurred his horse and moved toward the hill.

Chapter Three

Tracking at night can be difficult, even with a full moon, but Lilly did not realize she was being followed. The young woman's focus was speed. Max Thompson figured Lilly needed to get something done and then return to the Circle T before her father realized she had left the ranch.

As Thompson rode a safe distance from his prey, he remained unable to even speculate on the lady's motives for being out so late. Lilly had always been mischievous, but still a sweet kid. . . .

Max Thompson gave a whimsical laugh. A lot of time had passed since he really knew Lilly Tantrall. Why, she had been little more than a child when her father sent her off to that school in the East. Elijah had hated to do it. He missed his daughter very much. But Elijah's wife had died when the girl was eleven and the rancher had no idea how to raise a daughter.

Thompson halted his horse. Up ahead he could hear feet hitting the ground as Lilly dismounted from her palomino. They were on a slope, but not a steep one. The hill was large and trees were plentiful. The sheriff tied up his black gelding and proceeded up the hill on foot. He reached a clearing and spotted a cave with a large entrance. A flickering light suddenly ignited from within. The fire was not too bright. Lilly must have lit a lantern and kept it a good distance from the cave's opening. The girl had arranged a meeting with someone, but who and to what end?

Max slowly approached the cave entrance. He could hear Lilly's voice. She was nervously half-singing, half-humming a song. He moved closer to the entrance.

Cold iron pressed against the back of his neck, followed by a low whisper, "Say anything and you're dead." A gag was tied around Thompson's mouth. Another whisper followed. "Move. No tricks, or you die."

Max couldn't shake the feeling that he was about to die, no matter what.

The lawman proceeded down the hill, silently cursing himself. He had apparently been captured by a member of the gang he was trying to capture.

Thompson breathed heavily and kept his fear under wraps. He had always known that a lawman's slightest error could cost him his life. He hadn't given a thought to checking the area around the cave before moving in. It looked like that misstep was going to be deadly.

His lawman's instincts remained strong. The jasper who whispered the orders to him seemed to be trying to disguise his voice.

Thompson was forced into a grove of trees. The gag was removed from his mouth and this time the captor who gave the orders made no attempt to change his voice. He spoke in an almost jocular manner as he yanked off his hood. "I'll give you a moment to make peace with your creator, Sheriff. I always liked you. Sorry it's come to this."

"I'm already at peace with my creator." Max Thompson turned around and shook his head at the man who had a hood in his left hand and a six shooter in his right. "I never woulda guessed. You had me fooled. I must be gettin' old."

The unmasked outlaw laughed. "Gettin' old is a problem you're not gonna have, Max."

Chapter Four

Lilly Tantrall was benefitting from one of the advantages of being young, though she didn't realize it. The girl carefully looked in the large mirror that adorned a wall in her bedroom. Her eyes were bright, not betraying the fact that she had received little sleep the night before.

"Father won't suspect a thing," she whispered to her reflection.

The young woman then hurried down the stairs to the kitchen. She needed to help Kate with preparing breakfast. The task was a delicate one. Kate had been with the Tantrall family since before Lilly was born and had long ago ceased to be thought of as an employee. She was an honorary Tantrall. But age and a recent illness had left Kate frail and limited. Lilly needed to exert a lot of diplomacy as she helped the cook and housekeeper with the heavier tasks.

"Good morning, Kate!" Lilly sounded an upbeat note as she entered the kitchen.

"Mornin' child, sleep good?"

Lilly tensed up inside. Kate was a light sleeper. Did the cook hear her riding off last night or sneaking back into the house?

19

"Yes, just fine, how about you?"

"Oh . . . I slept good enough."

The ambiguity in Kate's response heightened the young woman's tension but she tried not to let it show. "I guess it's time for me to make myself useful. Lem promised he'd fix the kitchen pump this afternoon." She picked up a large bucket that resided in a corner of the kitchen. "This will be the last morning I need to fetch water."

"Child, I can do that!" There was an element of plea in Kate's voice.

"I know, but you have so much else to do, I'll be right back."

Lilly hurried out of the kitchen and headed outside. The pump was located near the barn and as she put down the bucket she could hear a horse's nicker from inside. The neighing sounded far too close to the door. Did one of the horses break out of its stall?

The young woman lifted the bar and opened the barn door. Immediately inside was a saddled horse. The animal didn't belong to the family, but it looked familiar. "This is Midnight," Lilly spoke softly as she petted the black gelding. "Sheriff Thompson's horse, what's—"

Lilly spotted blood on Midnight's saddle, then she saw the body on the floor.

"Sheriff Thompson!" Lilly Tantrall crouched over the body of the lawman. She felt for a pulse knowing there would be none. What lay in front of her was a pale corpse.

For in that sleep of death what dreams may come . . .

Those words that suddenly played in the young woman's mind were from Hamlet's soliloquy. Two years ago, Lilly had recited the famous speech in class. But when she came to "mortal coil" she had said "mortal soil." Sally Hendricks, who never liked her, shouted out, "Hamlet must not have taken a bath that day." The entire class erupted in laughter. Lilly had felt humiliated and angry.

The young woman now began to laugh as tears escaped the corners of her eyes. She continued to laugh hysterically as she ran from the barn. When she stormed into the house, she tried to shout for her father but her laughter morphed into a loud, terrified scream.

Chapter Five

As he approached the Circle T, Rance Dehner could see a large herd of cattle spread over flat grazing land. From a distance they looked like a dark cloud stirring restlessly on the ground. Elijah Tantrall's Circle T dominated the area around Capstone, Texas. Most of the other ranches were small ten head operations that survived by selling cattle to Tantrall.

As he rode into the ranch proper, he was received with suspicion. There were plenty of ranch hands around, all of them giving him hostile glares.

At the ranch house matters improved a bit. A large, broad shouldered man was talking with a very attractive young woman. The lady smiled at the newcomer as he approached. Her companion gave him an unfriendly glare, but at this point, Dehner was used to it.

"Good afternoon," the detective said, "My name is Rance Dehner. I'm here to see Mister Elijah Tantrall."

The broad-shouldered man continued to glare and the young woman continued to smile as she spoke. "I'm Lilly Tantrall and this is Lem

Donnigan, our foreman. You must be from the Lowrie Agency. I've never met a real detective before." The woman's voice exuded graciousness. She wasn't really all that impressed with Dehner's occupation.

Lem Donnigan was even less impressed. "I've knowed a few detectives. They were all crooked men looking for a crooked dollar."

Rance replied in an easygoing manner as he crossed his hands on the saddle horn. "From what I hear about Elijah Tantrall, he can sum a man up pretty fast. If I'm the kind of detective you're talking about, Lem, he'll be throwing me out of his house in a few minutes."

Lilly saw Dehner's reply as an opportunity to get down to business. "Please come inside, Mr. Dehner. Father ordered that you be brought to him as soon as you arrive." The woman put an emphasis on the words "father ordered." She seemed to be delivering a message to the foreman.

Dehner dismounted, tied up his bay, and followed Lilly into the house. The young woman walked him through a large, attractive living room complete with plants and a painting done by a renowned western artist. Dehner figured that those touches did not come from the ranch owner. A feminine hand was at work here.

"I apologize for the way Lem acted. He's usually welcoming to strangers," Lilly said.

"I understand how Lem feels, Miss Tantrall."

"Oh?"

They passed through the living room and started down a hallway. "I'm an outsider brought in to help. Whenever that happens, there is usually somebody who takes offense. Somebody who thinks he could have handled the job just fine."

Lilly looked thoughtful and paused a few moments before speaking again. "Yes, Lem has been father's right hand for several years now. He's the man father goes to when a special problem comes up. But Lem needs to realize that this problem is different. A lot different."

They stopped at the last room in the hallway. Lilly knocked on the door and opened it at the same time, moving her head inside. "Father, Mr. Rance Dehner of the Lowrie Agency is here to see you."

"Show him in!"

The moment Rance stepped inside, Lilly closed the door. Her retreating footsteps could be heard moving down the hall. The detective figured those steps were suspiciously loud. There was a theatrical quality about them: the steps of someone who planned on quietly returning and listening in at the door.

Elijah Tantrall stood up from his large desk and extended a hand. "Thanks for gettin' here so soon Rance. Good to meet you."

The two men shook hands as Dehner spoke. "I

had just finished up a case nearby when I got the telegram from Dallas. The boss said you wired him about a problem."

"Yep, I got a problem all right." Tantrall motioned for Dehner to sit in a chair that fronted the desk. As he did so, Rance gave the room a quick once over. The desk was a mess of papers and, besides the chair, the only other piece of furniture was a large sofa that sagged from plenty of use. Dehner surmised that the rancher often slept on that sofa after a long night of battling paperwork.

Tantrall looked scornfully at his desk as he once again settled in behind it. "Spent a good part of my life stayin' away from this kind of work. My wife, Connie, use ta do this stuff for me. Nothin' has been the same since she died."

For a moment, Elijah stared blankly at a wall. He had gone to a different location but quickly returned and looked directly at Dehner. "There have been several attacks on home-steaders around here recently. Started off with barn burnings, fences pulled down, that sort of thing. Then three days ago, an entire family, the Ashleys, were murdered in broad daylight."

"What has the local law done?"

"The law around these parts is Max Thompson . . . or was. Max was killed two nights ago while searching for the killers of the Ashley family. His body was dumped in my barn." Tantrall paused and pressed his lips together. Dehner realized that Max Thompson had been friends with the rancher.

Elijah Tantrall only needed a moment to get his emotions back in check. "Glenn Kagan, the head of the Homesteaders Association, is convinced that I'm responsible for murderin' the sheriff. The way he sees it, Max was my puppet but he suddenly grew a backbone and defied one of my commands. That's when I killed him."

Dehner made a sarcastic laugh. "And then you left the body in your own barn!"

"The way Kagan sees it, I'm a criminal mastermind. I put the body in my own barn ta make it look like one of the homesteaders killed Max and then tried ta frame me."

"Any notions as to the real reason the corpse was left in your barn?"

"None!"

"I take it you're not on good terms with the homesteaders."

Tantrall sighed deeply. "I've always been on the side of law. This country needs law. I want Lilly ta be able to settle here and have a good life. But—"

Dehner spoke softly. "The law is on the side of the homesteaders."

"Y-e-p. I've had a hard time acceptin' that. Pulled down one of Glenn Kagan's fences a while back."

"Did you apologize to Kagan?"

"No. But I paid for the damn fence after Max told me I had ta."

"What do you want me to do, Mr. Tantrall?"

"The new sheriff is Lucky Chandler. A nice kid. He made a fine deputy for Max and Lucky can take care of the town, handle the hard cases, that sort of thing. But he could be in over his head with tryin' ta find Max's killer."

"You want me to find out who is behind the raids on the homesteaders and that will also uncover the snake who killed the sheriff," Dehner said.

Elijah nodded his head. "Glenn Kagan has got a real bug in his ear about me. He's stirrin' up the other homesteaders. We ain't far from a land war."

"Any ideas about where I can start?"

"We're buryin' Max tomorrow mornin'." The ranch owner fussed with his hands before continuing. "After that, they're holdin' a town hall meeting where our new sheriff will talk some about how he plans to stop all the trouble."

"You want me to meet Lucky Chandler."

"Yep, but more than jus' that, it'll give you a chance ta scout the territory, get a feel for the people involved. You can see what happens when the ranchers and the homesteaders get together in a room . . . it could be right entertainin'."

"I'm looking forward to it."

"Fine," Tantrall's chair loudly scraped the floor as he got up. "Kate, our cook, will have supper ready in about an hour. I want ya ta stay here with us. We've got plenty of space." He walked with Dehner into the hallway, where he gave a friendly shout. "Lilly!"

"Yes, father?" Her voice came from the living room and dripped with casualness.

"Show Mr. Dehner to a guest room."

"Yes, yes, of course."

Rance gave the rancher a nod before walking swiftly into the living room. Lilly was perched on the end of a chair, sitting upright in almost military stiffness with both hands in her lap and both feet tucked as far under the chair as she could get them. "I'm sure you have some things in your saddle bags, Mr. Dehner, things that you will want to carry to your room."

"Yes, I do, Miss Tantrall. I'll fetch them right now."

Relief shot across the young woman's face. "Great! When you get back, I'll show you to your room."

Rance stepped outside of the house before Lilly could see the smile on his face. Lilly Tantrall was not good at deception. She had tried to conceal her feet but hadn't quite succeeded. She was in stocking feet. Dehner's earlier notion had been right. The young woman had taken off her footwear to avoid detection and then

28

returned to her father's office door to listen in.

But why? Dehner was purposely slow in retrieving his saddle bags. He wanted his hostess to have ample time to get her boots back on: best to let her think the trick had worked.

Chapter Six

Capstone, Texas stood as a typical dusty western town with the usual main street consisting of saloons and stores serving the needs of both ranchers and homesteaders. Rance Dehner noted that the gunshop had the street's most impressive storefront window and sign. That particular business was obviously thriving.

A town surrounded by ranches brings in a lot of drifters looking for work. A stranger in town was not an unusual sight. Elijah had pointed out a few people to Dehner at Max Thompson's funeral. Dehner circled around the well-dressed crowd, most of whom had also attended the funeral and were now congregating outside the Wet Dog Saloon where a town meeting would shortly take place.

Rance kept a close eye on Lilly Tantrall. He noted with amusement that he was not the only man doing so. But one young man seemed to have more luck than others. He was a boyishly handsome lad with dark hair and a pronounced limp. He didn't speak to Lilly but they exchanged intense glances and a few quick hand gestures.

A short, stout man with a handlebar mustache

shouted at the crowd from the boardwalk immediately outside the saloon. "We got all the tables
wiped clean for you; time to start the meeting."

Elijah suddenly appeared at Dehner's side and
pointed at the speaker. "That's Walt Goulding,
he's the mayor and the owner of the Wet Dog and
another saloon in town."

The crowd ambled into the saloon initiating a
strange procedure. Everyone stood around for
a few moments waiting for Elijah Tantrall and
Glenn Kagan to take their places. Elijah, accompanied by his daughter, ramrod, and Rance
Dehner, moved to the far right side of the saloon
where they sat down at a table.

After watching Elijah, Glenn Kagan moved to
the far left side of the Wet Dog and sat down.
He was accompanied by a woman and the young
man Dehner had spotted silently communicating
with Lilly outside the saloon.

The rest of the crowd then played follow the
leader: the ranchers sat on the right side of the
saloon and the homesteaders on the left. The left
side was far more populated.

Elijah had already pointed out Glenn Kagan
to the detective. Rance needed to confirm a
suspicion. "The two people with Kagan, are they
his wife and son?"

"Yes. Wife's name is Judith; the boy, Rory, is
their only child."

Dehner better understood Lilly's covert behavior

the day before. She was having a romance with the son of her father's enemy! *Romeo and Juliet come to Capstone, Texas,* Rance thought. He didn't find it to be a pleasant notion and decided to keep it to himself for the time being.

A man in his early twenties, medium height with sandy hair and a bushy mustache walked to the front of the bar and began to speak. "Most of ya know me, I'm Lucas Chandler, ever one calls me Lucky. I use ta be Max Thompson's deputy. Mayor Goulding has made me sheriff for the next sixteen months. After that, I'll have ta run for office like Max woulda had ta do."

The sheriff twirled the hat which he held in both hands and then continued. "Four good people have been killed hereabouts, ya all know that. But I jus' wanna say that I'll do ever thing I can to find the killers. And I won't be working alone. I'd like all of ya to meet my new deputy, Chet Harmon."

Chet's first day on the job got off to an awkward start. His knees knocked the table he was sitting at as he got up. One lady in the homesteaders' side of the saloon gave a painful yelp as Chet passed by.

"Sorry, ma'am, didn't mean to step on your foot."

The lady replied with a noble smile while others pulled their feet a safe distance from the new deputy.

"Chet Harmon, he's a good choice," Elijah spoke in a low voice, half to himself, half to the people at his table.

"How do you figure that?" Dehner asked as the tall, gawky young man made his way to the front.

Elijah continued in the low voice. "Ever one knows Max and I were friends and Lucky worshipped Max. Chet is the son of a homesteader, Frank Harmon. Lucky is showin' people that he ain't partial ta one side . . . he's tryin' ta show 'em anyways."

Rance didn't immediately share the rancher's optimism. "How is Chet with a gun and his fists?"

"Don't know," Elijah admitted.

Chet made it to the front of the saloon without inflicting any more injuries. He stood beside the sheriff and grinned nervously.

Lucky Chandler stared at the crowd with a look that bordered on being accusatory. "There's been a lotta talk in this town about the killings and how the law has been handling it. Let me say right now that we jus' buried one of Capstone's finest men. Max Thompson was a great sheriff; Chet and I will do our best ta be the lawman he was. If anybody's got something to say, now's the time. Let's hear ya."

Glenn Kagan sprang from his chair as if he had been waiting for this moment. "Sheriff, if you're really so interested in stoppin' the killin's maybe

33

you should take a look at the table now occupied by Elijah Tantrall."

Kagan pointed a finger at Rance Dehner. "It seems like Mr. Tantrall has added a hired gun to his payroll. There ain't no way that gunny could have knowed Max Thompson but he was at Thompson's funeral. Maybe he wanted to see how his own handiwork turned out. Maybe that hired gun has been around Capstone for a spell, we just ain't seen him. Maybe Tantrall knows a lot more about the Ashleys and Max Thompson gettin' killed than he lets on!"

Elijah shot up from his chair and faced his accuser. "Kagan is once again sayin' things against people that are just plain loco. The man he's yappin' about is named Rance Dehner. He is a detective from the Lowrie Agency. He's gonna do ever thing he can to help the law find who's behind the killin's."

Tantrall and Kagan remained on their feet, staring at each other intensely from across the saloon. Kagan's extended hand became a fist as he shook it at Elijah. "You don't seem to have much faith in our new lawmen, Tantrall. Maybe it's because they ain't your buddies the way Max Thompson was . . . poor Max . . . he got killed when he'd no longer lick his master's boots."

"That's enough, Mr. Kagan!" Chandler inhaled, bringing his anger under control. "No one's gonna bring down Max Thompson's name without proof."

Kagan turned toward Lucky Chandler, both hands now at his side. "Tell me, Sheriff, did Capstone's good citizen, Elijah Tantrall, tell you anything about this great detective he was set on hirin'?"

"I ain't had a chance to tell 'im," Elijah yelled. "Dehner arrived around supper time yesterday. This mornin' Lucky's mind was on the funeral. It wouldn't have been decent to discuss business right then."

"When did you get so all worked up over decency, Elijah?! You didn't care much about bein' decent when you had thugs knock over fences . . ."

Glenn Kagan paused for a moment as he tried to recall another travesty committed by his adversary. Frank Harmon took advantage of the silence and stood up. "I'd like to say something, Sheriff."

"Please do, Frank." The sheriff's abrupt reply to the question caused both Kagan and Tantrall to sit down.

Frank Harmon paused and fidgeted as if questioning whether he should have asked to speak. He swallowed hard and then began to make his point. "As most of ya know, Chet is my boy and I'm proud of him for agreein' to become a deputy when our town has so many troubles."

Murmurs of agreement arose from both sides of the saloon and there was light applause. Frank looked at his hands, then raised his head and continued. "But I ain't the only one who should feel that way." Harmon looked directly at Elijah. "Mr. Tantrall, your girl is doin' her family proud. She has helped some strugglin' homesteaders to keep their mouths above water. Some folks say you're not all that pleased with what she's doin'. I don't know 'bout that but I do know ya should think high of her, ever one else in this town does."

Frank Harmon sat down surrounded by loud applause from his fellow homesteaders. Dehner noted that the applause from the ranchers was cautious. Most of them were eyeing Elijah to see how he was responding.

Elijah didn't seem to be responding at all. He was looking at the table. Sitting next to the rancher, Dehner could see that his face was red but he couldn't discern why.

Elijah slowly stood up. "Thank you for speakin' the truth, Frank. I am proud of Lilly, damn proud!" He smiled at his daughter as he sat down.

Another, louder round of applause followed. Sheriff Chandler motioned for Lilly to stand up which she reluctantly did as she mouthed the words, "Thank-you" to the crowd and then returned to her chair.

A fragile sense of goodwill now pervaded the

Wet Dog Saloon. Lucky Chandler decided not to press his luck. "I think we've said all that needs ta be said. I'm callin' this meetin' to a close."

As folks slowly got up to leave, Elijah hurried Dehner to the front of the saloon and introduced him to the new sheriff and deputy. As he shook hands with the lawmen, Dehner eyed Lilly Tantrall who was graciously accepting kind words from people she had helped.

But Lilly was making quick work of it. She obviously wanted to leave the Wet Dog.

Dehner watched the young woman pass through the bat wings. "Good meeting you gents, I'll see you later."

The detective hurried out of the saloon in time to spot Lilly riding out of town. Rance's bay was tethered to the hitch rail in front of the Wet Dog. He untied his horse and began to follow Lilly Tantrall.

Chapter Seven

Lilly was easy to trail. The woman was riding fast. Another fresh set of hoof prints were close to those of Lilly's palomino. Near a large hill, she had stopped and joined with the other rider who was waiting for her there. Dehner didn't need to think very long on the identity of the other rider.

The detective carefully guided his bay up the hill, noting that the two people in front of him didn't require such caution. They had made this journey before.

Rance heard the whinny of a horse. He pulled up and dismounted, then guided his horse into a thick grove of trees and tethered him.

He quietly advanced up the hill on foot until he came to Lilly's palomino which was tied up to a tree beside a buckskin. Voices were coming from a cave which was only a few feet away. Dehner moved as close to the mouth of the cave as he dared and listened. He immediately recognized Lilly's voice.

"Please, let's not talk about it, Rory. I was so embarrassed."

"Ever one was clapping their hands for you. The whole town's loving you, almost as much as I do. And you deserve it! Didn't you tell me you're helping out another family later today?"

"Yes, I'm going to visit the Randalls."

"They speak high of you too, jus' keep your eyes and ears open, you'll find out I'm right. You got the whole town of Capstone loving you . . . what's wrong, Lilly?"

"You were right about something else," the woman answered. "That was a shot you heard three nights ago when riding up here. Whoever killed Max Thompson placed the gun right against his chest to muffle the shot."

Rory Kagan's voice lost its playfulness. "I tole you I came back the next day and found where it happened, down near the bottom of the hill; there was blood all over the ground."

"Poor Mr. Thompson, he looked . . ." Lilly paused and her voice wavered a bit as she continued. "Why would anyone do such a terrible thing, and why put the body in our barn?"

"Sheriff Thompson got killed 'cause he was getting close to finding out who was behind all the trouble in these parts. The body got dumped at your ranch to make your pa look like a killer, the man who ordered the Ashleys to be slaughtered like cattle. And I already tole you who—"

"Rory, I know your father is a hard man but I can't believe he's a killer."

The young man's voice quivered slightly. "There's something I never tole you."

"What's that?"

"This limp of mine, Pa gave it to me."

"What?"

"Happened when I was thirteen, me and Pa was building a fence. He tripped over a hammer he had jus' laid on the ground and I laughed. He picked up the hammer and hit me behind my right knee."

"I thought you fell off a horse."

Anger flared in Rory Kagan's voice, "That's what ever one thinks! Pa tole Doc Muller I fell offa horse. Pa even made it a big joke, 'that fool boy of mine, I ordered him to stay off that roan but he wouldn't listen.' The whole town laughed at me!"

"Did you tell anyone what really happened?"

"No. Ma saw it all."

"What did she do?"

"She yelled at Pa something ferocious, even slapped him, but . . . Pa beats her when she tries to stand up to him . . . beats her hard."

The young man's voice stopped and Dehner could hear the rustle of feet. Rory was pacing about the cave. When he spoke again his voice was higher and more intense.

"My Pa has gotta be the biggest man around: the man who always gets his way! You ever notice there's never been another election for head of the Homesteaders Association since Glenn Kagan took the job?"

"Well . . . no . . ."

"Pa threatens any man who even talks about another election. He wants to be king of this territory and he can't be as long as Elijah Tantrall is around."

Something resembling a gasp and a cry came from Lilly's throat. "Your father wants to start a war, doesn't he?"

"Yep. The way he sees it, there are a lot more homesteaders than there are ranchers. And the small ranchers ain't likely to risk their lives when it comes to gunplay. Both sides will bring in hired guns but Pa will have more people fighting for him."

"He wants to kill my father?!"

"Yep. Pa will then grab more land. He'll be rich and powerful."

"Rory, let's tell the sheriff about this, or maybe Rance Dehner."

"Wouldn't do no good. I ain't got no proof. And, you know, folks hereabouts don't take me serious. You've heard 'em call me gimpy."

"I take you seriously, Rory. I know what kind of man you are . . ."

Silence followed and Dehner knew what was happening inside the cave. He felt vaguely guilty. *Romeo and Juliet should be able to embrace without a detective eavesdropping.*

When the couple began to speak again, they talked of time passing quickly and the need to get

41

back to their homes. "When can we meet again, Lilly?"

"I don't know." The young woman gave a whimsical laugh. "Having a detective at our house does confuse matters. I'll leave a note in the usual place."

The abundance of trees on the hill made it easy for Rance to take cover before Lilly and Rory left the cave. The detective watched the couple as they mounted and rode off.

After they were gone, Dehner ran to his bay. He needed to get back to town and the two lawmen quickly.

Chapter Eight

Johnny Randall, age eight, sat on his pony and looked into the beautiful face of the woman standing beside him. The boy stammered a bit as he spoke. He was both happy and nervous.

"Thank ya, Miss Lilly, you're the most wonderful person in the whole world!"

Lilly Tantrall laughed and once again felt embarrassed. This seemed to be her day to receive compliments. "Don't thank me, Johnny, thank your mother and father. I just did what they asked and hid the pony at our place. Your parents wanted to surprise you on your birthday!"

Johnny smiled but a trace of doubt skittered in his eyes. Special gifts were rare for a boy living on a hardscrabble farm. His folks were poor and he knew it.

John Randall rode up on the chestnut he had just retrieved from the barn. "OK son, let's take a ride together!"

The older Randall gave Lilly a look of gratitude. She responded with a smile. Lilly knew how hard it was for the men to accept help from a woman. But John Randall would not let pride keep his son from having a happy birthday.

"Lilly, I don't know what to say . . ."

Cynthia Randall's voice was soft and the two men hiding in a dry wash about fifty feet on the right side of the farm couldn't hear her. But that didn't worry them. They were worried about her husband.

"He's probably going to ride around the barn and then head toward us," Rance Dehner whispered as he motioned backwards with his thumb. "Let's get back into the trees."

Dehner and Deputy Chet Harmon quietly left the wash and made it into the grove of scraggly trees where their horses were tied up. They stood motionless until John Bradley and his son rode by on the opposite side of the wash. By the time the two horsemen made it back to the house, Lilly had departed and Cynthia was inside fixing supper.

"Ouch!" Chet snapped.

"Quiet," Dehner's response came in a whisper.

Deputy Harmon lowered his voice. "Sorry, I backed into a tree branch and poked my neck."

Dehner spoke as he watched John and Johnny enter their house. "No harm done, they didn't hear you. Let's get back to the wash."

"Wash," Chet scoffed. "Ain't been any water in this river for goin' on eight months."

After leaving Lilly and Rory, Dehner had ridden back into Capstone where he shared his notions with the new sheriff. Lucky Chandler sounded skeptical as he slowly replied. "Guess you could be right but it don't seem likely." He scratched his head. "Then again . . . look, I'll send Chet with ya, he'll be finished with his round soon. I think it's sorta important for me to stay here in town."

Chet and Rance were now back in the wash. Chet definitely shared his boss's skepticism.

"I can't see how you figger there's a connection with Lilly's visit to the Ashleys and them getting killed."

"I don't think there was a connection but there may be one soon."

"Huh?"

"You were at the meeting this morning," Dehner said. "You saw how people responded to Lilly Tantrall's visits to the homesteaders. There was a real feeling of goodwill in the air."

"Yep, but . . ."

"Someone is trying to start a war between the homesteaders and the ranchers. What happened this morning couldn't have made that person very happy."

"Guess not, but there ain't a thing he can do 'bout it."

"What if the Randall place gets attacked today, the day Lilly Tantrall paid a visit?"

Chet gasped in a load of wind and exhaled it slowly. "Seems ever body is on edge these days. They'd probably come up with some fool notion of Lilly somehow setting up homesteaders to be killed."

Dehner nodded his head. "All that goodwill would vanish and this area would be thrown into a bloody land war."

"So you think the Randalls are gonna be attacked today?"

"Probably tonight. This time the gunnies will hold off until dark. It's a lot easier for them that way."

Rance gave the area a quick look. "We have a good position here." He pointed at a large grove of trees about twenty yards in front of the house. "Those trees provide better cover than the ones behind us. The killers will probably hide there and get ready before moving in."

"How many d'ya suppose there'll be?"

"At least three, thugs like to work in a group."

"Lordy." Chet's voice made that word sound like a prayer.

"Are you sorry you became a deputy?"

Chet Harmon fell quiet, giving the question careful thought. When he spoke, his voice conveyed certainty. "No, ain't sorry at all."

Chet wasn't sorry but he was restless. The sun set too slowly for him. "Dehner, are you one of those folks who make a big deal 'bout the sun coming up and going down?"

"I don't follow you."

"Some folks like to jaw 'bout the sun looking

46

great in the morning or when it sets. Max Thompson tole me there's a place in Dallas where you jus' walk around and look at pictures people have painted. A lot of those pictures are of the sun coming up or going down. Why bother to make a picture of that? You see it ever day!"

"Well . . ."

The erratic whispered conversation continued until the sun had long vanished. A partial moon provided enough light for Dehner to spot the shadow of a horse and rider moving toward the large cluster of trees near the front of the house.

The detective pointed at the shadowy specter as it took cover in the trees. "This attack has been well planned."

"Whatta ya mean?"

Dehner replied as another shadow moved through the night. "They're gathering one by one. That's quieter than everyone riding up at once."

"We move now?"

"Yes. You go to the left end of the house. I'll go to the window and warn the family, then take the right end."

Keeping low in a jackknife position, Chet moved quickly to his location. Rance took one last look in the direction of the enemy. Two other riders were approaching at a fair distance from each other.

Dehner made a fast run to the back window of the house, silently giving thanks for the hot night. The window's shutters were open. He looked into the window and the end of a Sharpes rifle.

"Don't move mister. Call your friend over here. I spotted him runnin' by."

Rance tried to speak in a calm matter, though he had to talk fast. "My friend is the deputy sheriff. Your home is about to be attacked by night riders. Get your wife and son to where they'll be safe. Use that Sharpes to fire from the front window. The deputy and I will take each side of the house."

"How do I know you're tellin'—"

The sound of pounding hoofs sounded from the front of the house, accompanied by loud screeches. John Randall pulled in his rifle and shouted, "Cynthia, take Johnny and go into the bedroom, now!"

An array of shots blared from three hooded riders that rode toward the house. As Dehner took his position, Chet fired at the invaders and took one down.

The night riders were stunned. They had been firing into the air, trying to instill a paralyzing fear into their victims. They had anticipated a few shots from the front window but no more.

One of the riders carried a fiery torch. Dehner's first shot knocked the target off his mount. The outlaw hit the ground and let go of the torch which landed near his horse. The sorrel panicked and lifted onto its back legs, coming down hard on its rider.

The third outlaw wheeled his horse in an attempt to escape. But a flash from the front window made the invader's body go rubbery. He clung to his horse for a few moments, then collapsed to the ground as the animal galloped off.

Dehner carefully eyed the three bodies now lying on the ground to ascertain if there was any movement. One outlaw began to crawl toward a gun that lay only a few feet away from him. Chet Harmon stopped him with two shots.

Rance sighed and shook his head. That outlaw would have been valuable alive. They might have been able to get some information out of him. Now he would be just one more wasted life that ended in a nameless grave.

The detective and the deputy left their positions. Dehner was not surprised when Chet moved immediately toward the man he had just shot.

"My first shot only wounded this jasper, guess I needed to finish the job." Chet's false bravado carried a strong current of anguish. Rance was certain that the deputy had just killed a man for the first time.

Dehner said nothing as he checked the other two outlaws who were also dead. This was no time to lecture the young deputy on proper procedure.

All three outlaws had worn flour sacks over

their heads. The detective carefully removed those hoods. He knew none of the dead men and yet he did. Their faces all reflected violent lives. These were men who lived by brutalizing and often killing innocents. The detective took no joy in their deaths, neither did he mourn them.

"Sorry, Mr. Dehner, I saw ya at the meetin' this mornin'. I shoulda recognized ya right off but guess I got too wound up when I heard footsteps in the back of my house." John Randall spoke as he stepped off the front porch of his home. He was carrying his Sharpes.

"I understand, Mr. Randall, is your family OK?"

"Yes." The homesteader looked at the deputy who was now approaching the two men after disappearing to the side of the house for a few moments. Dehner knew why he had disappeared.

"I'm mighty grateful to you and Mister Dehner, Chet. How'd ya know those snakes were gonna attack us tonight?"

Chet's voice now rang with a reckless abandon. "Thank Rance Dehner, he figgered—"

"I just thought the deputy and I should ride around after sundown to spot anything suspicious. We had some good luck."

Chet Harmon picked up the cue, "Ah . . . yep."

Dehner led his two companions as they checked the torch which now was just a large, glowing ash and then took a close look at the outlaws. Randall hadn't seen the invaders before. The faces did look vaguely familiar to the deputy. "Seen 'em leaning against the bar at the Wet Dog a few days back, jus' took 'em for saddle bums."

Randall noticed the twitchy look in the detective's eyes. Somethin' botherin' ya, Mister Dehner?"

"Maybe. I could be wrong but I thought I counted four riders—"

A horse bolted from the trees in front of the house. The rider was slung low to avoid getting hit by gunfire. As the steed raced from the three men, John raised his Sharpes.

"No!" Dehner pushed the rifle's muzzle toward the ground, as he drew his Colt and fired harmlessly into the air.

"Why'd ya do that?" Randall asked.

"Whoever is on that horse thinks we tried to stop him." Dehner holstered his gun then continued. "Too late to track him now, but I'll be up early and get on his trail. He could be valuable."

Curiosity filled the emptiness that had been in Chet's eyes. "Why would that jasper be more valuable than them other owlhoots?"

"He didn't take part in the attack," Dehner answered. "That probably means he's a boss of some kind. There could be another reason."

"Like?" Chet asked.

"Maybe he's someone we would recognize." Dehner paused and then continued. "Yes, I plan to be up very early tomorrow."

Chapter Nine

The sky's darkness was being replaced by an iron gray as Dehner spoke in a low voice to Chet Harmon. "Before you ride back into town, stop at the Circle T. Tell Elijah what happened last night. Tell him to keep Lilly away from the homesteaders for a while . . . tough as that might be."

"What should I tell him 'bout you?"

"The truth. I'm going after the fourth man who tried to attack this place last night."

Rance and Chet were standing on the porch of the Randall's farmhouse. Both men were drinking coffee which Cynthia had prepared for them. They had slept outside, the ground being softer than the floor of the Randall's small house. The detective's bay was saddled and standing only a few steps away.

John Randall approached the two men carrying a canteen he had just filled up at the water pump. He handed the canteen to Rance as he stepped onto the porch. "That owlhoot may be headin' for the border. I know this place looks dry but the land gets really barren just a few miles south. Stop at ever creek ya can find."

Dehner started to say that his own canteen should do but settled for saying, "Thank you." John felt he owed the two men for what they had done the night before; refusing the canteen would have been an insult.

Cynthia bustled onto the porch holding a small bag; Johnny trailed behind her. "I've fixed some biscuits for you, Mister Dehner. I wish you'd stay for breakfast."

"I'd love to ma'am but I'll have to let Chet eat my portion." Dehner gave a two fingered salute, then mounted and rode off.

John had been right. The attacker's trail did head south. At first the tracks reflected the hard pounding of a fast retreat. But the rider had slowed down once he felt safe. Whoever Dehner was tracking knew the area well and was handling his horse with care.

Sunup made the trail easier to follow but brought increasing heat. By midday the ground was becoming rough and stony dotted with brown patches of dead foliage. Large, ragged boulders dominated the area like a conquering army.

Dehner's shirt was soaked with perspiration by the time the sun began to weaken. Sundown made Rance consider Chet Harmon's statements the day before. The retreating orb splattered blood red on the boulders. It was an edgy sight, and there was nothing beautiful about it.

"I think most artists would pass this place by,"

Dehner said to his bay while patting him on the neck.

As night moved in, the detective figured his prey had crossed the border into Mexico. He began looking for a place to camp. Distant lights along with the tinkling of music and laughter caused him to think again.

Dehner rode directly toward what appeared to be a small town. Enough lights emanated from the place that Rance could spot two figures at the entrance. They appeared to be sentries.

As he drew closer, the notion of two sentries was confirmed. Both men carried rifles and looked at the newcomer with suspicion.

An overweight man with bloodshot eyes did the talking. "What's your name, stranger?"

Dehner gave a cynical smile. "Joe Jones, I can be Sam Smith if you prefer."

The suspicion lowered in both of the sentries' eyes. "Looks like you've been ridin' pretty hard today, Joe."

"Yep. Things got a mite uncomfortable where I was."

"How'd ya hear 'bout Devil's Due?"

"A friend told me . . . a friend who you could say is in the same line of work I am."

The sentry guffawed and motioned for Dehner to ride on into town. As he made his way down the noisy street, the detective felt relieved that he had been able to get past the guards. But his relief was short lived. Rance Dehner didn't know the story behind Devil's Due but he knew he was riding into trouble.

Hosea Rimstead bowed his head in prayer before he stepped into the Fast Dollar Saloon. He would need the Lord's protection. Beau Rawlins, the owner of the saloon, had him pegged as a trouble maker. After finishing his prayer, Hosea felt more confident than ever that God was directing his steps and Beau Rawlins be damned.

So to speak.

Hosea stepped into the saloon and saw the woman he had come for. Gail was standing up from a round table and wishing two cowboys luck as they ambled toward a roulette wheel.

All of the men inside the Fast Dollar were called cowboys, even though there hadn't been a ranch in the area around Devil's Due for at least three years. The clientele at the Fast Dollar, along with most of the population of the border town, consisted of outlaws on the run from the law.

"I need to talk with you," Hosea spoke to Gail as she was walking back to the bar.

The expression on the woman's face could have been anger, hope, or sadness, maybe a combination of all three. "I told you never to bother me again, Hosea."

"Yup, you told me a lot of things."

"Hosea . . . please."

Hosea looked about anxiously. So far, no one was paying them any mind. He had to keep it that way. "Look, I got me some money. I want for us to go upstairs. Just to talk. But I'll pay you just as if . . ."

Gail pressed her lips together and looked down. "OK."

As they moved toward the stairway, Hosea noted that the Fast Dollar looked like a typical western saloon. The second floor was horse-shoe shaped with plenty of rooms where girls made money for their boss. The stairway on one side of the saloon was dented and scratched. A large wagon wheel chandelier containing kerosene lights hung from the ceiling.

"After we talk, I'm gonna do some preachin'," Hosea said in a loud whisper. "Warn these people about the comin' judgment."

"These people don't want to hear nothin' you say! These jaspers have themselves enough troubles with the law here on earth. They don't need to hear about some law ridin' down on 'em from the sky."

The couple reached the second floor and entered one of the rooms. The room was blue, dirty and didn't have a window. The only furniture in the place was a bed and a small side table which contained a vase and a lantern that was already lit.

"There ain't enough space here to turn around in," Hosea groused.

"People don't come here to turn around."

"Guess not."

"Say what's on your mind, you're payin' for it." Gail tried to sound harsh but couldn't quite manage it.

"Gail, you need to come back to me and be my wife!"

"No!"

"Can't you see, woman, you're disobeyin' the Almighty. God sent me to Devil's Due to—"

"The Almighty didn't send you here, you got lost! You were headin' for Capstone but confused north and south. Are you sayin' the Almighty can't tell north from south?"

"I'm sayin' the Lord works in mysterious ways."

"Sounds more stupid than mysterious to me."

"Well, if that don't—" Hosea began to pace about the room and collided with the bed. The jolt seemed to calm him down. His voice became low. "The first time I saw you, I knew you were special. I could tell you felt somethin' like that about me."

Gail smiled wistfully and Hosea noticed she was wearing the same red dress as the first night he had seen her. Long black hair flowed over her bare shoulders. The girl stood close to Hosea's six feet, with a pretty face highlighted by blue eyes, a small nose, and a small mouth.

Hosea's voice became pleading. "Can't you see,

it's just like the Hosea in the Bible! He married a . . . well . . . a saloon girl, and then she left him and went back to bein' . . . well . . . a saloon girl, but she returned to him and the second time around it went fine."

"I've read the story. Felt sorry for the girl."

"Why?"

"She was named Gomer. That's awful."

"Well, back in those days, they did get some fool notions about names. Look, what's happenin' to us is what happened to those folks in the Bible, only you and I ain't never got hitched. Now, if ya will jus' go along with—"

"I can't go along, Hosea. I thought I could. I wanted to. But, if I married you, I'd have a husband who preached in the streets and got laughed at! I can't live like that. Go away, Hosea. Let me be what I am."

"No! The Lord wants you to—"

"Stop tellin' me about what God wants! You've got no right—"

The door sprang open. A large boned, blond haired man stalked in. "What's goin' on? Well, it's the sky pilot. You've been told to stay out, Hosea."

"You don't order me, Lars Olsen. The Lord is on my side!" Hosea took a step toward the intruder. Olsen laughed contemptuously, his eyes gleaming with anticipation.

Gail took a few fast steps that placed her

between the two men. The young woman put a hand on Hosea's chest. "Please Hosea, leave now. Lars Olsen will kill you and enjoy doing it!"

Hosea gently moved Gail away. "David defeated Goliath with a sling shot. Reckon I can whup this owlhoot with my bare hands."

"Is that right, Preacher Man? Well, I'm gonna count to ten and then I'm gonna beat you up, real good. Yep, maybe I'll do like the girlie says and kill you. So, that Lord of yours better get busy and strike me down now!"

Olsen began to count. Hosea felt trapped. He knew the Lord wasn't going to strike Lars Olsen down. The Divine just didn't work that way. But all that would take some complicated explaining and Olsen wasn't much for complicated explanations.

Hosea Rimstead realized, too late, that his challenge to Lars Olsen had been an attempt to impress Gail with his manliness. In other words, pride . . .

"Ten!" Rimstead ducked but it didn't work. A fist slammed into Hosea Rimstead's face. He heard Gail's screams as he plunged to the floor.

"Please Mr. Olsen, don't hurt him bad!"

"Okay, Honey. But you just remember, when Lars Olsen does someone a favor, he expects a favor in return. Understand!?"

"Yes." Even with the sharp knife of pain slashing across his head, Hosea could see the look of resignation that made the young woman's face appear haggard as she responded to Lars Olsen.

Olsen bent down and grabbed Hosea by the collar of his frock coat. He dragged him out of the room and shouted from the second floor, "The preacher man is all tuckered out after spendin' time with one of our girlies. I gotta help him downstairs."

The entire saloon exploded in laughter as Lars Olsen dragged Hosea down the stairway. When they arrived at the bottom, Lars picked Hosea up while still holding him by the collar. "He was prayin' for a miracle all the way down. Kept askin' the Almighty for a body made of iron!"

More laughter followed as Olsen walked a stumbling Hosea to the bat wing doors and tossed him out. "That girlie wants nothing to do with you! Stay away or I'll kill you!"

Rance Dehner carefully eyed Devil's Due as he continued to ride through the town. There was obviously no law here. Devil's Due seemed to be a place where outlaws gathered like worms crawling into a coffin.

Dehner halted his bay. His attention went to the Fast Dollar Saloon where a blond haired man had just tossed another man into the street.

The man who had been tossed got up quickly, then staggered a bit. He was thin and wiry. His voice was surprisingly deep. "Your days of killin' and hurtin' are numbered, Olsen. Judgement is comin' on you, comin' on this whole sinful town!"

Dehner tied his horse at the hitch rail outside the saloon. He went unnoticed by Olsen, who laughed as he stepped back into the Fast Dollar. The detective approached the deep voiced man who was brushing dirt off his trousers.

"Are you okay, friend?" Dehner asked.

"I'm blessed, if that's what you mean." He extended a hand. "The name is Hosea Rimstead. I was named after the Old Testament prophet."

Rance observed that the man looked like a prophet, with a thick black beard that, to some degree, masked his youth. A close look at his face revealed that Hosea was in his early twenties. "My name is Rance Dehner. I was named after a rich uncle my father was trying to borrow money from."

To Rance's surprise, Hosea laughed good naturedly. "Did it work?"

"No. I disappointed my daddy the day I was born."

Hosea smiled broadly. "Guess we all got our burdens to carry."

"Reckon so. You look like a man who has acquired some recent burdens."

"Yup." Hosea touched his face lightly and quickly retracted his hand. "I got what was comin' to me."

"What do you mean?"

"I challenged a man much bigger than me to a fight. In other words, I put the Lord to the test. You ain't supposed to do that. It never turns out good. Enough about my troubles, what brings you to this cesspool of sin, Rance?"

"I'm tracking a killer."

"Well, you came to the right place, plenty of 'em here."

"I had one specific killer in mind."

"What's he look like?"

Dehner grinned and gave a slight laugh. "I can't say. He was wearing a hood last time I saw him, hiding his identity. But I'll know him when I see him." The detective pointed toward the Fast Dollar. "This place looks like the biggest saloon in town. It's a good place to start."

"You could be headed for trouble, I'll go with you."

Dehner was surprised by Hosea's offer which sounded genuine. The man was wearing a black frock coat, black trousers, white shirt and no gun.

"You're not armed, Hosea. Going back into a place like the Fast Dollar without a gun . . . after being thrown out . . . well . . . you could be setting up another test for the Lord."

"Good point. But listen, you won't be alone, brother. I'll stay right outside here and pray for you."

"Ah . . . thanks."

Dehner stepped onto the boardwalk and glanced backwards. Hosea's head was bowed and his hands clasped together. His whispered words sounded intense. Rance couldn't decide if the man was loco or genuinely devout. He reckoned that was a question for later. The detective pushed open the batwings, entered the Fast Dollar Saloon and realized immediately that he would need Hosea's prayers.

Chapter Ten

"Well, well, I thought the Fast Dollar was a decent place; looks like it's got a problem with rats. I tole yuh we'd meet again, Rance Dehner."

The voice came from a tall, husky man leaning against the bar. Dehner spoke with mock friendliness. "Jake Matson, the last time we met you tried to kill me. That didn't work out. Maybe you should buy me a drink and we can talk things over peaceable like."

"Not hardly."

Rance had to play this situation carefully. He had tangled with Matson on an earlier case. The outlaw had slipped away vowing revenge on Dehner. Now Jake Matson posed an overwhelming threat. He knew Dehner was a detective. That knowledge could amount to a death warrant in a place like Devil's Due.

Matson's arm hovered over his Colt .44. A path cleared between the outlaw and the detective. Dehner's eyes were focused on his immediate adversary. He didn't see the familiar face only a few feet behind him. The figure stepped quietly away from Dehner and began to move up the stairway. But he didn't head for any of the rooms used by the Fast Dollar's patrons. He hurried to the office of the man who ran Devil's Due.

"Ya know, Dehner, I should be a rich man right now." Matson's face was pale and his breathing fast. "Ya had ta get in the way and ruin all that."

"You need to be more philosophical about such matters, Jake. You're just not the kind to get rich."

"It's time for some payback, Dehner."

"Gentlemen!" A voice bellowed from the second floor. "Let's carry out this dispute in a proper manner."

A well-dressed man hastily made his way down the stairs. "Jake, we always look forward to seeing you in action, but this stranger looks like a man who can handle a gun."

"No, Mr. Rawlins, he's jus' a jasper who tricked me once."

Rance knew he'd have to shoot it out with the gun for hire. And Dehner had to kill Jake Matson before he told a town of outlaws that Rance Dehner was a detective.

Dehner thrived on moments like this. Never did he feel so alive as when he stood only moments away from possible death. The detective also hated himself for such primitive emotions. Sitting beside a campfire with only his own thoughts, he would often wonder what kind of man would pursue a life of violence and death. Was he any better than the outlaws he tracked?

But such thoughts were for later. For now he kept his eyes and mind riveted on the man who wanted to kill him and the man who had injected himself into the duel.

Beau Rawlins had a moon face and the beginning of a double chin. In an almost regal manner, Rawlins strutted to where he stood between the two adversaries and addressed Dehner. "Welcome stranger; we always appreciate a gent who brings a little entertainment to Devil's Due, right folks?"

Laughter filled the saloon. Dehner reckoned similar laughter once filled Roman coliseums. The detective noted that Jake Matson's arm moved away from his gun and his eyes filled with resignation. The outlaw was ready for the kill but he would now have to wait. In Devil's Due, Beau Rawlins ran the show.

Rawlins nodded toward the outlaw. "All of us admire Jake. Those who don't admire him end up dead!"

More laughter followed the remark. Rawlins smiled and held up his hand to quell the noise. "But none of us know how fast the stranger is with a gun. That does make things interesting." Beau pointed toward one of the saloon girls who was standing a safe distance from both Dehner and Matson. "Polly, get behind the bar and help Fred take bets. I suspect most men will bet on Jake but some of you jus' might want to take a chance on the stranger. In the most unlikely event that both men kill each other, the house takes all. Step up gentlemen, and place your bets!"

Pandemonium followed, as men stormed the bar and Rawlins ordered the swamper to move tables toward the walls. Beau Rawlins was also giving whispered orders to other men. The saloon owner had worked at sounding casual when he proclaimed that the house would take all if both gunfighters ended up dead but Dehner knew there was nothing casual about it. He would have to kill Jake Matson and how many other gunnies?

Close to fifteen minutes passed before the betting closed. Dehner noted that during that time Jake Matson returned to the bar, grabbed a bottle and glass he had been working on when Dehner entered and poured himself another drink. Would the booze help or hinder the outlaw's draw? Rance didn't know.

"Looks like everyone has put down their bets, time for the competition to begin!" Rawlins beamed a smile at the patrons. He stood in front of the bar. Dehner was on his right and Matson on his left. Both men were several feet away from the saloon owner but he spoke to the two adversaries as if he were a referee giving instructions before a boxing match.

"Gents, you can see that I have cleared plenty of space. I'm going to ask the two of you to stand at opposite ends of the bar. That way, the customers can find a place where they'll be safe from a stray bullet . . . only a precaution mind you, I'm sure neither one of you will miss."

This time the laughter sounded frantic. As Dehner followed the instructions, he saw that Lars Olsen was positioned behind Matson, close to the crowd lining the wall beside the bat wings but far enough away to ensure that a bullet from his gun would have an easy path to its target.

The detective didn't bother trying to spot the gunman who would be aiming at Jake Matson in the event he won the fight. Rawlins's plan was simple but there was no reason it couldn't work. When the shooting started there would be plenty of screams and hollers. The few people who did notice that a shot was fired by a gunman in the crowd would remain silent. Devil's Due was Beau Rawlins's town.

Beau scooted to the front of the bat wings where he put an arm around the woman he had earlier called Polly. "I'm gonna ask the Queen of the Fast Dollar to count to three. You gents slap leather on three, not before."

Polly's eyes were bright with happiness. She was relishing the attention. "One, . . . two, . . . two and a half, . . . THREE!"

Rance drew his Colt, fired and dropped to the floor in one fast motion. A bullet whined over his head but Dehner was sure it didn't come from Jake Matson's gun. Matson's body was twirling as he clutched his weapon in one hand, struggling to get off a shot before he went down."

"Fire at Matson!" A familiar voice boomed loudly as a red spear cut across the saloon.

Dehner's second shot sent Matson's body into a spasm before knocking him to the ground. The detective looked past his victim to see another body crumpling to the wood.

Rance then noticed a pair of highly expensive boots coming his way. As he looked up he saw a friend adorned as usual in a white suit with the suspiciously wide sleeves that the gambler always demanded in his attire.

"Stacey Hooper, we seem to be getting into a rut," Rance spoke as he got to his feet. "The last place we ran into each other was also a saloon and, as I recall, there was a gunfight."

"Well, as Ecclesiastes instructs us, 'There is nothing new under the sun.' However, that does not mean life is always predictable. Don't holster your Colt yet, my friend."

No one in the Fast Dollar heard this conversation. They were too busy gathering around the two bodies that now occupied the floor of the saloon.

"Matson's dead as a door nail!" A voice bellowed over the clamour.

"Just like old Marley in Dickens's Christmas Carol!" Heeding his own advice, Stacey kept his gun in hand. "But now we do know, Rance, that your two shots found the mark. Let's see how I did with only one humble bullet."

Hooper and Dehner walked across the saloon to where a circle of men were looking down while casting quick glances at Beau Rawlins whose face was dark with anger. Stacey spoke in a bright, upbeat voice. "I have saved the Fast Dollar's reputation, Beau. Some misguided employee obviously thought you'd be impressed if he killed Dehner and, thus, set up the situation where the house took all. Of course, such lowly undertakings are far beneath you."

Rawlins's upper lip moved above his teeth. He started to speak and then stopped. When he finally spoke his voice carried a barely controlled anger. "You killed Lars Olsen. He was one of my most dependable gun . . . one of my most dependable men."

"You have my deepest condolences," Stacey smiled benignly.

The anger flooding the face of Beau Rawlins increased in fury. The saloon owner started to speak to Stacey, then suddenly pointed to the corpse and spoke to the men standing around him. "Get this outta here. The swamper will have to clean up the mess."

As Rawlins stalked off, Dehner spoke quietly to his companion. "Let's leave, Stacey."

"In just a moment friend, first I have some pleasant business to attend to."

"What's that?"

"Why, to collect my winnings. I'm one of the few people in this establishment who bet on you."

Both men kept their guns in hand while in the Fast Dollar. The move seemed to be only a precaution. Activity in the saloon quickly resumed, indifferent to the gunplay that had just taken place. But there were eyes that remained on Dehner and Hooper as they left the saloon.

The two men were greeted by a shout of, "Praise the Lord!" as they stepped outside onto the boardwalk.

"I forgot you were out here, Hosea!" Rance holstered his gun as he spoke to the bearded young man.

"Good thing the Lord never forgets where no one is!" Hosea's voice remained a shout. "I've been out here praying. Of course, I heard the gunfire and all. The Lord answered my prayers and protected you and Stacey."

Rance's face reflected surprise. Stacey Hooper laughed mischievously as he put away his gun. "Yes, Rance, I am friends with this present-day prophet. We met the day I arrived. He was preaching in the street and I became an audience of one. Together we are functioning as a team . . . sort of."

Stacey glanced at the sky and continued to speak. "Hosea is right. The Almighty is with us tonight. He has provided a bright moon and dazzling stars. May I suggest a ride out of town?"

"Where do you have in mind for us to go?" Rance asked.

"As you may have already surmised, Hosea has me pondering the wisdom of the Good Book: 'Vanity of vanities; all is vanity.' Indeed. Some unfortunate fool thought he could start a large ranch in this God forsaken . . . excuse me, Hosea . . . part of Texas. He had a rather daft plan for bringing in water. It didn't work out. Now all that is left is a dilapidated ranch house and some line shacks. However, it does suit the present needs of both myself and my prophet friend. Come gentlemen, we must not dally much longer!"

As Stacey and Rance stepped into his sight, the figure in Beau Rawlins's office quickly let go of the curtain that covered a large window which looked out on the town. He whispered a curse for only thinking about the light on the desk now. He extinguished the light then returned to the window, more confident of not being spotted.

The figure laughed in an almost gleeful manner. Dehner and Hooper were riding out of town with the religious moron. Rawlins had been growing increasingly unhappy with Hooper and had talked about killing the religious idiot who tended to be a trouble maker. Tonight, Beau Rawlins would kill three birds with one ambush.

The figure again let go of the curtain. Happiness waved over him as he lay down on the office sofa. That damned detective had obviously trailed him after the shooting at the Randall place. But all that hard riding had come to nothing; Dehner failed to spot him in the saloon.

Now, Beau Rawlins was gathering a group of men for the kill. More important, Rawlins had agreed to help pull off a bigger job: one which involved the good folks of Capstone, Texas.

A deep sigh of satisfaction came from the man plotting a land war. He'd sleep for an hour or so, and then head back. He couldn't be gone for too long.

He laughed once more before falling into a contented sleep.

Chapter Eleven

The three men were some fifteen minutes out of town when Rance Dehner looked backward. "I see a dust cloud moving toward us. Can't tell how many riders there are."

"I anticipated this," Hooper's voice was thick with amusement. "Beau was quite disturbed by tonight's turn of events, though I don't know why. He seems to have quickly engaged a band of ruffians to dispatch us to that promised land in the sky Hosea tells us about."

Rance Dehner felt uneasy. "I could be the reason Rawlins is taking action."

A smirk appeared on Hooper's face. "I rather thought that was the case."

Dehner gave his companions a chagrined look. "I hear laughter from our pursuers, they don't seem to mind if we hear them coming."

Stacey continued to look amused as he tilted his head. "At this time of night, the entire population of Devil's Due is inebriated. Our would-be assassins are no doubt feeling giddy about their evil assignment."

"Satan's brew has been the ruin of many a soul," Hosea lamented.

"Yes. But tonight Beelzebub's bottles may be our friends." Stacey turned around in his saddle. "They aren't making very good time. Let's ride a bit faster. There are a few things we need to get done before we confront those villains."

They spurred their horses into a gallop over the flat, dismal land. The few bushes and trees they rode past were withered and bent, as if this portion of the territory was a monument to death.

Stacey pointed to a dark patch which lay in front of them. "Up ahead!"

They reined in at a slight ravine containing five crooked trees huddled together as if trying to comfort each other. An abandoned shack stood several yards away. Stacey spoke as the three men dismounted. "This is one of the few spots that offers shade in the daytime: an obvious location for a line shack."

"What do you have in mind, Stacey?" Rance asked.

Stacey hastily opened a saddle bag, pulled a wax object out and held it up for his two companions to see. "I plan to light one candle rather than curse the darkness. You gents tie up the horses."

The gambler ran to the dilapidated structure. True to his word, candlelight could soon be seen through the shack's one small window. The light revealed only a small portion of the rickety table it perched on. Stacey ran back to his companions and hastily explained his plan. The three men waited in the darkness of the trees. Rance and Stacey held Colts. Hosea Rimstead was now armed with a Winchester he had pulled from the boot of his saddle.

The sound of approaching hoof beats mingled with the laughter Rance had heard earlier. Both sounds came to a stop. Whispering could be heard, followed by a couple of guffaws. A moment of total silence followed, then gunshots were fired at the cabin as four men rode toward it. Two of the men were firing pistols and two carried carbines. Splinters of wood exploded from the shack as a storm of bullets pierced it. One of the carbines blew a hole under the window of the shack. The candle's light flickered erratically as it dropped to the floor but didn't go out.

The four men pulled back and admired their destruction, as if they had just pulled off a dangerous military maneuver. The flame that still flickered inside seemed to hypnotize them for a few moments.

"Think anyone is still alive in there?" One of the outlaws asked, his voice slurred a bit by alcohol.

"Na. They're all dead, or close to it. But let's move in slow."

Later, it would occur to Rance Dehner that what happened next may have looked funny if there had been a bystander around to watch. The four outlaws dismounted and began to move slowly toward the shack. As they did so, Stacey, Rance and Hosea moved from the shadow of the trees into the moonlight and advanced quietly toward the backs of the owlhoots.

"Freeze and drop your guns, gentlemen!" Stacey shouted. "Failure to comply will result in immediate death."

The outlaws did what they were told. Although they couldn't see him, there was no mistaking the voice of Stacey Hooper. One of the jaspers spoke, his voice trembling, "You gonna shoot us down like dogs?"

Stacey Hooper's laugh conveyed a genuine sense of fun. "I believe we can avoid such a grotesque approach. No gentlemen, I believe this occasion calls for a touch of whimsy."

Hosea Rimstead and Stacey Hooper entered the dirty ranch house with easy familiarity. Rance Dehner scanned the well-built house that, at first glance, appeared empty of everything except dust, bugs and rodents.

Stacey picked up on his friend's somber mood. "The West is a place where men dream big and fail even bigger."

"And some men die along with their failed dreams," Dehner added.

Dehner's statement seemed to spook Hosea. "You don't think those four jaspers we left tied up back at the line shack will die, do you?"

"No." Rance replied quickly. "They'll get out of their ropes sooner or later. We ran off their horses but left the outlaws one canteen. If they use it wisely, it will provide enough water for them to find the horses and get back to town."

Hosea turned to Stacey. "Hope you didn't mind my objectin' to your idea about takin' away their boots. That just didn't strike me as bein' Christian."

"Not at all, Hosea!" Stacey responded cheerfully. "I appreciated the theological insight."

Rance looked about the deserted house, noticing blankets and large patches of disturbed dust. "Have you fellows been living here?"

"Indeed," Stacey said. "A gambler is always in danger from those misguided souls who believe they were cheated. Devil's Due poses a special peril because there's no law."

"A street preacher's also got problems," Hosea added. "Jaspers think it right funny to push around a man of God, jus' like they did in the Old Testament days."

"So this is home sweet home," Rance said.

"Yep," Hosea replied. "We take turns sleepin'. One of us is always on watch."

Dehner looked at a portion of moonlit floor where a spider was attacking a small insect. "What can you tell me about the charming town of Devil's Due, Stacey?"

"Devil's Due was started about two years ago,

the product of Beau Rawlins's warped mind. Criminals on the run pay Rawlins in order to stay in the town. Rawlins provides them with saloons and living accommodations to their liking as well as a town free of individuals who might capture them for the reward. Such a set up would be difficult to find in Mexico."

"Yup," Hosea added, "but if the law does show, and that don't happen much, some folks take a ride south before they can be arrested."

Dehner heard a scampering sound on the floor and caught sight of a rat running along a baseboard. He wondered, casually, if rats attacked spiders. The detective turned his attention back to his companions. "How did you end up in Devil's Due, Stacey?"

"Beau and I are long time chums, though I suppose 'associates' would be a better word. Beau hired me to play for the house."

Stacey's reply had been too quick and neat. The detective looked dubious. "You're going to a lot of trouble for this job of yours; come on, there's more to it."

"Correct, my friend," Stacey's voice took on a new vibrancy.

Rance knew he was being set up but didn't know what to do about it. "So, what is the real reason you are in Devil's Due?"

Hooper held his chin high, "I am here on an assignment for the Texas Rangers!"

Dehner's chin dropped. "What?! . . . Stacey, you've got to be joking!"

"Not at all. The Rangers want to close down Devil's Due with a minimum of bloodshed. For that, they need someone who is willing to serve as a spy. Would either of you gentlemen care for a cigar?"

Both of his companions responded with a quick, "No, thank you."

Stacey bit off the end of the cigar and spit it onto the floor. The rat Dehner had spotted earlier heard the noise and disappeared into his hole in the floorboard.

"The Rangers want me to keep an eye out for any hard evidence that Beau Rawlins has committed a serious crime for which he can be arrested and prosecuted." Stacey looked dreamily at the cloud he blew from his mouth. "There is a special beauty to cigar smoke in the moonlight, don't you think?"

"No!" Dehner didn't give Hosea a chance to respond. "Stacey, you're not giving me the whole story, why are you doing all this for the Rangers?"

The gambler faked a surprised look. "Why, it's my civic responsibility!" He turned to Hosea. "You'll have to forgive Rance. A hard life of sin in a fallen world has left him calloused and cynical."

Dehner stared at the gambler. "Stacey,—the truth—or something reasonably close to it."

The odour from Hooper's cigar began to compete with the other odours in the house. Dehner admitted to himself that the stogie's smell was an improvement. "Well . . ." the gambler's tone turned light, as if he was reviewing facts of little importance. "I was a very minor partner in a business venture that went awry."

"What happened to the major partners?" Dehner persisted.

"They're all in jail," Stacey replied.

"But the Texas Rangers have an extensive knowledge of your . . . ah . . . activities." Dehner felt relieved to be getting at the truth. "They knew you and Beau Rawlins were chums, so they offered a deal: you help the Rangers find evidence that will allow them to arrest Rawlins and therefore close down Devil's Due, or you go to prison."

Hooper flicked an ash from his cigar. "Crudely stated, but you have the gist of it."

"From the way he was acting tonight, I gather Beau Rawlins is becoming suspicious of your motives for being in Devil's Due," Dehner said.

"He's suspicious all right," Hosea spoke up. "But for the wrong reasons. Beau thinks Stacey is tryin' to take over Devil's Due and run the town hisself. He mighta spotted you as a gunman Stacey brought in to help with the dirty work."

"I won't be worrying Rawlins much longer. I'm riding back to Capstone at sunup."

Stacey pointed his cigar at Dehner. "Since you have demanded the complete truth regarding my presence in Devil's Due perhaps you could tell us what brought you to this desolate location."

"Fair enough." Dehner gave his companions a quick summary of his work for Elijah Tantrall, including the attack on the Randall place and how he had trailed the surviving gunny to Devil's Due.

"Fascinating!" There wasn't a trace of sarcasm in Stacey's voice. "Your story fits perfectly into a theory I have been pondering of late."

"What's that?" Dehner asked.

"I think Beau is getting ready to shut down Devil's Due. Yes, the operation has made him some money but it's fraught with peril. The customers are of a low class and don't always pay their bills. I think Beau is getting ready to move on."

Stacey blew another cloud of cigar smoke but this time didn't comment on its esthetic value. "I've noticed that, of late, several denizens of Devil's Due vanish for a few days and then reappear. Perhaps the villains who are plaguing the good yeomen of Capstone are being provided by Beau Rawlins."

Dehner nodded his head. "And someone is serving as a go between . . . and maybe more than that. Whoever it is panicked when the attack on the Randalls failed. He came back here and made some new plans with Beau Rawlins. He's probably headed back to Capstone by now. My ride here was a waste of time."

"Don't say that, Rance!" Hosea shouted. "Why, you ridded this place of Lars Olsen. That was a blessed removal!"

"Indeed!" Stacey raised his voice to match that of Hosea. "And before this matter is settled we may have to send a few more hardened souls to a well-deserved perdition."

Chapter Twelve

Stacey Hooper opened the door of Beau Rawlins's office and stepped in without knocking.

Rawlins sat at his large desk, putting flame to a cigar. "Why ain't you downstairs, making money for the house?"

"I will be shortly, but there is a disruption going on below which, I believe, requires your attention."

Rawlins waved the matchstick until the flame went out and a line of smoke dissipated in the air. "I don't handle that kind of stuff anymore. Get Lars Olsen."

"Alas, Mr. Olsen is unavailable. As I am sure you will recall on reflection, Lars Olsen was killed last night."

"Yes, Yes." Beau dropped the matchstick into a small box of sand beside his desk.

"Don't be hard on yourself, Beau. An important businessman such as yourself is bound to lose track of petty details."

Rawlins's voice became defensive. "I gave George Drago Olsen's job but then changed my mind. I needed to send Drago to—" The saloon owner stopped and then spoke in a clipped manner. "I needed him to do something else."

Hooper feigned indifference to his boss's statement. "Perfectly understandable but nevertheless there is trouble downstairs and there is no one with appropriate authority present to deal with it."

Beau mumbled curses as he got up from the desk and stepped out of the office. Stacey followed him to the stairway but no further. Rawlins didn't notice.

The saloon owner was scared. His statement that he didn't "handle that kind of stuff anymore" was a total deception. Beau Rawlins had never allowed himself into a situation involving fisticuffs.

At the bottom of the stairway, Hosea Rimstead was blocking one of the saloon girls who wanted to come upstairs with a customer. Beau's fright eased a bit. Surely the religious moron wasn't much of a threat. Still, Rawlins pushed back his coat and ran a hand over the gun strapped to his waist. He wouldn't allow that fool preacher or anyone else to hit him.

The main floor of the Fast Dollar was unusually quiet. Most of the customers were focusing their attention on Hosea whose voice boomed over the saloon. "What's goin' on upstairs is of the devil. I ain't lettin' you keep dancin' to Satan's tune, Gail."

Laughter and mock cheers waved across the

Fast Dollar. Rawlins beamed a fake smile and waved to his customers as he made his way down the stairway and decided on his approach: a crazy preacher didn't merit direct action by the man who owned the town. He had hired hands for such trivial tasks.

Rawlins stopped when he was on the last stair, towering above Hosea. "OK, Preacher Man, enough of your sermons. Get!"

"My orders come from the Almighty, not you, Beau Rawlins!"

This time there was only a tinkle of laughter. Everyone waited to see how Rawlins would react.

The saloon owner gave a loud, theatrical laugh, followed by a motion to two men standing across the room near a roulette wheel. "Buck, Charley, hate to pull you away from the fun but this sky pilot is causing more trouble than he's worth; kindly escort him out."

Buck took quick strides toward Hosea, Charley followed right behind him. "Don't ya worry none, Mr. Rawlins," Buck shouted gleefully. "This is gonna be a lot more fun than bettin' on the wheel."

Gail's customer bolted from her side and disappeared into the crowd. The young saloon girl took only a few steps away before stopping and turning around. Her face contorted with fear. She knew Buck and Charley. They were violent men who wouldn't hesitate to beat Hosea until he was dead. They would view this as an opportunity to take the place of Lars Olsen.

Hosea didn't look at the woman he loved. He was preoccupied with sizing up his two opponents. The evangelist had encountered them before. They were hard thugs but not the Goliath Lars Olsen had been. Buck stood at below average height, fast but not very smart. Charley was tall but overweight and slow.

As his adversaries approached, Hosea took several steps toward them, shouting, *"Arise O Lord . . . for thou hast . . . broken the teeth of the ungodly."* He smiled at the two ungodly gents now only a few feet in front of him. "I was quotin' from Psalm Three."

Buck looked confused. "Ain't no gawd broke my teeth."

Hosea's smile appeared to sweeten. "Guess that means I gotta do it."

The preacher smashed a fist into Buck's mouth. Specks of blood spurted from Buck's lips as the owlhoot staggered back and fell.

Hosea ducked the first punch from Charley. As the preacher stepped back to avoid Charley's second swing the crowd's shouts and laughter resounded through the Fast Dollar. Beau Rawlins made his way quietly back to his office, almost unnoticed.

In the style of a boxer, Hosea danced around

Charley landing a blow on his left eye. He then feigned another attack to the head, followed by a sharp punch to his adversary's mid-section. The fat man bent over, Hosea was about to deliver another blow to Charley's head when he heard Gail's voice scream out, "Behind you!"

Hosea turned just in time to dodge the Remington which missed his skull by inches. Buck was back on his feet and seeking revenge. As Hosea stepped away from both of his attackers he noted that a splotch of red now covered Buck's lips and chin making him look like a grotesque clown.

But a clown with a gun: Buck pointed the six shooter at him as Charley advanced with both hands clenched into fists. Hosea made a desperate attempt to even the odds if only a little.

"You two fellas need to use a gun to stop one preacher! I guess two against one ain't good enough odds for you."

Both aggressors froze and glanced at each other. The pause was only for a moment. Both men felt they had been humiliated and only a quick and total retaliation would gain back their respect.

Buck's voice quivered with anger. "You're a fer piece from Sunday school, Preacher. Let me show ya how things git done in Devil's Due."

The outlaw fired a shot near Hosea's feet causing him to jump backwards in an almost comical manner. Gail screamed but the rest of the saloon exploded in laughter.

Adrenaline pumped through Buck. He was now in charge, making folks laugh at the man who had knocked him down. "My, Preacher, ya sure can jump. Ya must be tryin' to jump up to the big pie in the sky ya always babble 'bout!"

Buck fired another shot near Hosea's feet, forcing him to jump backwards towards the bat wings. "I'm gonna help ya git to the pearly gates, Preacher. Soon as we git outside, I'm puttin' a bullet in your head. Doin' it here would be impolite what with makin' a mess on the floor and all."

Gail frantically screamed for the outlaw to stop while the rest of the Fast Dollar patrons laughed and shouted encouragement at Buck. Hosea blocked it all out of his mind as he concocted a desperate scheme to save his life.

The preacher deliberately executed a comical jump as another bullet burrowed into the floor. Hosea noticed that Charley was laughing hard and becoming increasingly careless. Charley's gun remained in its holster and the outlaw was moving in closer to the funny jumping man who he now regarded as harmless.

Charley is plannin' to push me through the bat wings, the preacher thought.

One more bullet and one more jump proved Hosea right. As he reached the bat wings,

Charley's right arm shot toward him. Hosea grabbed the arm and twisted it as the two men plunged through the doors and hit the boardwalk outside the Fast Dollar.

They rolled over and off the wood planks, landing beside the hitch rail in front of the saloon. Explosive sounds filled the air as the Fast Dollar patrons ran outside to enjoy the entertainment. Hosea paid them no heed. His attention was now on the heavy-set man who was on top of him.

Hosea jammed a fist into Charley's throat. The large man fell over and Hosea tried to grab the gun from his holster but Charley rolled away from him.

A shout rang over the two fighters. "Git away from him, Charley, I'll put a bullet in him."

"I'm disappointed in you, Buck. Your fighting techniques are very unsportsman like. You would never have made the boxing team at Oxford."

"Wha—" Buck turned around.

Stacey Hooper slammed a fist into Buck's face and followed with a blow to the side of his head. The outlaw dropped his gun and crumpled to the ground unconscious.

Stacey scooped up the gun and pointed it at Charley. "On your feet, sir! Your involvement in this vile affair proves you are also a disgrace to the noble sport of physical combat. Where are the horses belonging to you and Buck?"

Charley wavered but managed to get to his feet.

He tried to answer Stacey's question but only a choke emanated from his throat. He nodded his head toward the hitch rail.

"Excellent," Stacey proclaimed as he pointed the gun downward. "I see that your friend is regaining consciousness. Help him onto his mount and then the two of you are to ride off and never disgrace this town again with your presence."

Charley managed a scratchy protest. "But we paid—"

"Leave!"

Charley obeyed but it was a long process. Getting Buck onto his feet and onto a horse took a while. By the time the two men were riding out of town the Fast Dollar patrons had shuffled back inside the saloon. Only Gail remained outside with Hosea and Stacey.

Stacey holstered Buck's gun in his belt as the two thugs vanished from view. "I apologize for my tardiness in providing help, Hosea. After looking through Beau's office, I hid in one of the rooms upstairs which, fortunately, was not in use as most of the customers were preoccupied with the entertainment being provided below, just as I had planned. I watched Beau return to his office, but waited until I was sure no one's eyes were glancing upwards before heading downstairs."

"That's OK," Hosea replied, "Did you find anythin'?"

Stacey shook his head. "Alas, no. Rance is certain that someone in Capstone is partnering with Beau Rawlins. He trailed that person here but couldn't locate him. Finding that someone could be beneficial to both the detective and myself. But our adversary is no fool. I couldn't find any written communication between Beau and his mysterious coconspirator in Beau's office."

"So, we still don't know who Rawlins is in cahoots with."

Hooper sighed before he spoke. "Yes, Hosea, that does summarize it rather well."

Gail's eyes widened with confusion. "Are you two pulling off some scheme together?"

"Yes," the gambler answered, "And your discretion in this matter will be greatly appreciated. You see, a Mr. Rance Dehner, the gentleman who terminated the employment of Lars Olsen last night, is interested in deposing Beau Rawlins. Hosea and I share his noble ambition. Beau has little regard for either Hosea or me. Thus, your silence in this matter will be most advantageous in helping us to achieve our worthy goals."

Stacey's words did not help Gail's confusion. She patted her hair nervously while talking to the gambler. "Sure, but, I don't understand, if Beau don't like you, why does he keep you on?"

"There are two reasons, both relating to the condition of original sin Hosea frequently brings

92

to our attention. Number one, I make money for the house, which appeals to Beau's greed. Number two, Beau, being a crook himself, is suspicious of everyone. To fire someone he suspects of wrongdoing would leave him without a single employee."

Hosea glanced briefly toward the Fast Dollar. Noisy revelry had resumed inside the saloon and no one paid heed to the threesome in the street. The preacher spoke intensely to Hooper. "What you say is right but if Rawlins finds out you're in cahoots with Dehner and the Texas Rangers, he'll have you killed sure."

"The Texas Rangers!" Awe, respect, anger and few other emotions not easily classified flashed across Gail's face as she looked at Hosea. "You and Stacey Hooper are working with the Texas Rangers?!"

"Yep! Well . . . I'm helpin' Stacey who's helpin' the Rangers. And Rance Dehner is a detective with the Lowrie Agency in Dallas."

The saloon girl pressed her lips together as anger began to win out over other emotions. "You mean . . . that big show you just made of not letting me go upstairs with a customer, all that was just for some job you're doing? You were getting Rawlins out of his office so Stacey could look through it?!"

Hosea began to gesture erratically with both arms. "No, well, yes but that was only a part of it. What you're doin' is a sin, Gail. You're sinnin' against God and man. The Lord will forgive you if—"

A loud squeak sounded from the Fast Dollar. All three people standing outside turned to face Polly who was standing between the bat wings.

"Get yourself in here right now!" Polly's voice snapped whip-like at the saloon girl. "You ain't making no money standing outside jawing with those two."

"Don't do it, Gail," Hosea gripped the woman's arm. You don't want to return to a life of sin."

Gail started to turn around and again face Hosea but she suddenly stopped and forcibly removed the preacher's hand from her arm. Polly stood back and gave the saloon girl some room as she reentered the saloon and vanished into the garish light.

Chapter Thirteen

Rory Kagan entered the kitchen cautiously. His mother, Judith, appeared nervous as she cleaned the breakfast dishes. But then, his mother often looked nervous ever since that day seven years back.

Rory had been thirteen when he and his father were repairing the small corral which stood to the right of their house. Glenn Kagan had placed a hammer on the ground to inspect his work and, moments later, tripped over the hammer. Rory laughed.

Glenn Kagan cursed loudly and picked up the hammer. Terror overcame the boy as he realized his father's intent. He turned to run but the tool slammed against the back of his knee sending him sprawling onto the earth.

Stepping out of the barn which faced the house, Judith Kagan had witnessed the entire incident. She ran to her son and crouched over him as he twisted in pain.

The woman began checking her son's injury, then looked at the man glowering a few feet away. "You monster! Doing something like this—"

Her husband's voice was a low growl. "Shut up, you!"

Judith angrily sprang to her feet and took several decisive steps toward her husband. "I won't shut up. I'm leaving you, Glenn, and taking Rory with me. And when folks ask why, I'll tell 'em the truth. Glenn Kagan is a no good coward who—"

Kagan brutally slapped his wife's face. Judith stumbled backwards but didn't fall. She inhaled, let out a breath that sounded like a hiss, then charged toward her husband and backhanded him across his stubbled cheek.

Glenn Kagan's eyes were wide with shock. He looked around as if trying to recall his location and identity. His mouth trembled and, for a moment, Rory thought he was going to cry.

But only for a moment: Kagan's face turned the color of fire as he clenched his hand into a fist and punched his wife. Judith screamed as she hit the ground near her son. The woman stifled her cries as she watched blood drip from her lips.

"You unnerstand now, not to talk back to your man?!" Glenn shouted.

Something flashed in his mother's eyes which Rory couldn't comprehend but admired. Judith Kagan wasn't defeated yet. She slowly began to get back onto her feet. "I understand not to talk back to you, Glenn. As for not talking back to a man, a real man, I guess I'd know more about that if I was married to one."

Her husband's anger was inflamed, which didn't surprise Judith. Those words had been employed as a distraction. Glenn Kagan took two fast steps toward his wife, indifferent to the rock she had picked up.

Judith swung the stone, hitting Glenn on the side of his head. But Judith Kagan was still reeling from the first blow she had absorbed and the swing was weak. Rory watched in horror as his father yelled vile obscenities at his mother and then for the second time, rammed a fist into her face.

This time, Judith collapsed onto her son, hitting his injured leg. Rory cried out in pain.

"I'm sorry, son." Swollen lips slurred Judith's words. The woman lovingly caressed Rory's head. "We'll get you inside, then go for the doctor."

"You do that, wife," Glenn said. "But if he asks you 'bout them bruises on your face, you tell him you fell down while working in the barn."

Judith glanced at her husband. She closed her eyes briefly before nodding her head. "Put your arm around my neck, Rory . . ."

A few months later, on his fourteenth birthday, Rory's mother had tried to talk with him about his father. "He's always had to think of himself as being an important person and, I suppose, there's always been a touch of the bully in him. But Glenn's changed a lot. Don't know why exactly . . . well, yes I do . . . he didn't use to drink so much . . ."

A strong bond was formed between mother and son, a hatred for Glenn Kagan being the centerpiece of that bond. Despite her hard life, Judith remained an attractive woman. Rory had noticed that when they went to church together on Sundays, always without his father, several widowers at the Capstone Community Church went out of their way to be cordial to her.

But Judith Kagan stayed where she was out of love for her son. There seemed to be an understanding between the two of them that once Rory could strike out on his own, his mother would divorce his father.

More recently, there had developed another, somewhat playful understanding between them. Rory was certain his mother knew he was seeing Lilly Tantrall. She had caught the meaningful looks and hand signals he had exchanged with Lilly. On one Sunday, riding in the buckboard back from church, Judith had commented, "Elijah Tantrall's daughter has certainly blossomed into a beautiful woman."

"Ah . . . yes," Rory had replied.

They had both laughed together. Now, Rory felt he was letting his mother down by remaining at home. He was twenty and it was time to act.

"Something on your mind, Son?"

Judith's question pulled her son back into the immediate moment. "There's a man here who says he wants to see Pa."

"What for?"

"Claims he wants a job," Rory answered.

"Well, Glenn might need an extra hand . . ."

Rory lowered his voice to a whisper. "He don't look like any farm hand to me, I think he's a gunfighter."

The kitchen door banged open. Rory and his mother were not surprised. That was the way Glenn Kagan always entered a room.

"What're you two jawin' 'bout?" Glenn Kagan's voice resounded with anger as it almost always did.

"There's a man outside lookin' for a job," Rory said.

His father gave a harsh laugh. "I need me an extra hand, you never seem to be 'round when work needs doin'."

Judith spoke firmly. "Rory needs time away from the ranch."

Her husband ignored the remark. "Where's this fella?"

"On the front porch," Rory answered. "Only I don't think he's a sodbuster; looks more like a gunny to me. I think you should send him on his way."

The farmer's eyes brightened, "What you think

don't carry much weight around here, boy."

Glenn Kagan left the kitchen and headed for the front door. The man who stood on the porch outside didn't disappoint him. He stood at slightly over six feet, broad shouldered with a heavy build, a scraggly brown beard and a Colt .45 tied low on his hip.

"Are you Glenn Kagan?" the stranger asked as Kagan stepped onto the porch.

The farmer smiled politely, a rare act for him. "Sure am, what can I do for you?"

"I think it's more a case of what I can do for you. The name's George Drago, I fix things."

"What kind of things?"

"W-e-l-l, a rancher 'round here name of Elijah Tantrall has hired himself a gunslick called Rance Dehner. Seems Tantrall thinks he owns this territory and is gonna use Dehner to prove it. From what I hear you're the only man hereabouts who has the guts to do somethin' about it."

"How do you plan to help fix things, George?"

"You jus' leave that to me."

Chapter Fourteen

Lem Donnigan leaned on the bar of the Wet Dog Saloon and, against his better judgment, asked for another drink. The sun was almost gone and the evening card games would be starting soon. He needed to keep his wits sharp.

He gazed at the mirror behind the bar and studied his own dour face. "Damn that woman," he whispered.

Donnigan knew he should be happy with his life. He was ramrod of one of the most prosperous ranches in the area. Elijah Tantrall was a great boss, couldn't ask for better, yet . . .

The foreman reckoned it had been about two years back when he fell in love with Lilly Tantrall. She had been home from that school in the East and he had trouble talking to her, until the end of summer when she seemed to start enjoying his company. But then, she returned East.

Now, Lilly was home for good. And she still talked so educated-like. She was polite enough to him but . . .

Lost in his sorrowful thoughts, Lem didn't notice the stranger who entered the saloon, approached the bar and ordered whiskey.

"Your name Donnigan?" The stranger shouted.

Lem turned his head slowly toward the man standing about five feet away from him. "Ah . . . yep . . . I'm Donnigan."

George Drago didn't give his name. This wasn't going to be a friendly conversation. "Figgers, ya look like a dog to me."

"Wha—"

"Ever one says you're Tantrall's lapdog. Ya fetch whenever he gives the order."

"You're loco."

"I guess it ain't such a bad life," Drago continued. "Tantrall must toss ya a bone now and again."

Lem knew the stranger was prodding him. He didn't know why but Donnigan could tell from the Colt tied low on the stranger's hip that he was being braced by a hired killer. He tried to ease himself out of danger.

"You're new in these parts, mister. After you're here a spell, you'll see things different."

Drago ignored the remark. "I hear old Elijah has a right pretty daughter. Tell me, does she smile at ya and pet your head when ya have been a good dog?"

A powerful air of tension fell over the saloon. Donnigan couldn't allow an insult like that to pass. If he backed away, the news of his cowardice would spread like a poisonous weed across the territory. Besides, he loved Lilly

Tantrall and resented her being talked about by a hired gun.

"You don't know what you're talkin' about, mister. I think you need to shut up."

George Drago gave a satisfied smile. He had accomplished his goal to push Donnigan into a gunfight he couldn't win.

The killer took a few steps away from the bar. "Make me shut up, Donnigan."

Lem knew he was about to die. Everything seemed so crazy! He was about to be gunned down by a man he hadn't even seen until a few minutes ago. The foreman moved to where he faced his adversary directly. He tried to keep his voice steady. "Your move."

"What's goin' on here?!" Sheriff Lucky Chandler shouted as he streaked through the bat wings of the Wet Dog Saloon.

Drago smiled at the lawman. "Jus' a little dis-agreement, Sheriff. I'm new in town and this here gent don't seem to care much for strangers. Tole me I had to vamoose."

"That's a lie, Lucky." Bewilderment waved across Lem's face. "This jasper braced me for no reason."

Chandler eyed the newcomer carefully. "What's your name stranger?"

"George Drago."

"Drago, I've never known Lem Donnigan to rawhide nobody. I think you're lyin'."

The gunfighter quickly took in the situation, remembering the instructions he had received at Devil's Due. This move hadn't gone as he had hoped. But he was getting good money and there would be other openings. No sense in going to jail and he didn't want to kill a star packer . . . not yet.

"Well, Sheriff, if ya say Lem's a good man, I'll take your word for it. Maybe there was jus' a misunderstandin'." Drago turned toward the barkeeper. "Tell us, apron, didn't ya think maybe Lem here had tole me to leave town?"

The gunfighter's cold gray eyes bore down on Omar, the barkeeper. Omar shrugged his shoulders nervously and stared at the floor. "Yep . . . I can see how maybe you might have thought Lem had said something like that . . ."

George Drago turned his head back to the sheriff. "Ya see, nothin' here but a little misunderstandin'." He sauntered toward the bat wings. "This is a nice town. Think I might stay a spell."

After the gunfighter departed, Lucky Chandler took Lem to a table in a distant corner of the saloon. He needed to get the truth about what had just happened and he didn't want to embarrass Omar, who he knew felt bad about lying to cover Drago's account.

After hearing the story, Chandler drummed his fingers on the table. "Sounds to me like Glenn

Kagan has hired a gunfighter to do some killin' for him. We're closer than ever to a land war." He patted Lem on the shoulder. "Watch yourself. I need to check around town to make sure Drago doesn't get into any more misunderstandin's!"

Donnigan remained in the saloon for another twenty minutes or so. Omar half-apologized to him for backing the gunfighter's lies; Lem said to forget it. Newcomers were told about the almost gunfight and everyone wanted Lem to tell it from his standpoint.

Lem didn't enjoy being the center of attention. He turned down the invite to join in for a game of poker and left the saloon. The ramrod walked aimlessly through the streets. He knew Lilly would hear about what happened in the Wet Dog Saloon. The story would hardly make him appear the hero. He had needed the sheriff to rescue him.

Donnigan realized the most important thing in his life was what Lilly Tantrall thought about him. "Damn that woman," he whispered for the second time.

Chapter Fifteen

"This is awful, Goldie," Lilly's voice was almost a whine as she spoke to her palomino. "Tonight is the last secret meeting. Tomorrow, I'm telling Father everything."

The horse replied with a nicker which, to Lilly, sounded like a strong expression of doubt.

"I mean it, Goldie," the young woman hastily responded. "If for no other reason, I'm not too far from being caught. I think Rance Dehner suspects something and Lem may also be suspicious. He's been acting strangely lately."

As she rode toward the cave where she was to meet with the man she loved, the young woman reflected on how these secret, late night rendezvous used to seem so exciting and romantic. She and Rory were a present day Romeo and Juliet: two star crossed lovers hindered by a senseless feud between their families.

But the bitterness that divided Capstone, Texas was real. Good people had been brutally murdered. She and Rory needed to stop playing childish games and do what they could to bring peace to the area.

She again spoke to Goldie. "I guess there's nothing childish about this meeting."

A few hours earlier, Lilly had ridden to what she and Rory called their "secret tree," a bushy cottonwood located reasonably close to the Tantrall ranch and the Kagan farm. She checked the low hanging branch which served as their private mail drop. The letter she found there was short and alarming:

Pa has hired a gunfighter. Must see you tonite.
Rory

Goldie, now familiar with this journey, began to ascend the hill which held the cave where Lilly and her boyfriend would meet. The horse slowed as it approached a familiar clump of trees.

Lilly dismounted, twirled Goldie's reins around a tree branch, then pulled a candle and a box of matches from one of her saddle bags. She lit the candle, returned the matches to the bag, and proceeded to the cave.

She entered the dark cavity carefully. Once inside there was no need for her to bend over. She made her way toward a lantern she and Rory kept on a small ledge in the cave. This task usually fell to Lilly. Unlike Elijah Tantrall, Rory's father had no real schedule. Alcohol made Glenn Kagan's life, and the life of his family, erratic and unpredictable. Rory had a hard time sneaking out. Lilly always arrived at their rendezvous first.

"Poor Rory," the woman said aloud as she lit

the lantern and placed the candle beside it. "He has such a hard life."

"Now, what are ya getting yourself feeling all sad 'bout, honey gal?"

Lilly turned abruptly and faced a large man with a threatening sneer and a threatening gun on his hip. Panic surged inside her, which she immediately quelled. "Who are you?"

"That's what I like honey gal, ya being nice and social like. My name's George Drago, I work for Mr. Glenn Kagan."

"You're the gunfighter Rory's father hired!"

"That's right, ya see, Mr. Kagan don't trust his son much. I followed him 'round a bit, read that note he left for ya in the tree. Followed him again tonight." Drago nodded his head toward the left. "Ya kin find him sleepin' under a tree nearby."

"What did you do to Rory?"

"Nothing much. Not like what I'm gonna do to that fool your Daddy calls a ramrod. I damn near killed him a few hours ago but the sheriff butted in. I plan to finish the job soon."

"You're a monster!"

Drago laughed and began to move toward the woman. "Guess you're right, honey gal but ya know, this monster can make a woman like yourself feel real good."

Lilly knew she had only one chance to stop George Drago. Her first move would have to work. She grabbed the lantern and swung it at her adversary. The glass cracked against Drago's belt buckle. The gunfighter yelled in pain as a flame touched his shirt and skin.

Lilly ran out of the cave as Drago bent over and slapped the fire out before it could crawl up his shirt. He shouted a curse and ran from the cave.

Outside Drago was tackled. He hit the ground on his side and screeched in surprise as he saw his attacker. "What the hell!?"

The gunslick pushed his adversary away and scrambled to his feet. "Who in blazes are you, mister?" George Drago bent over, his hand hovering near the weapon on his hip.

"The name is Rance Dehner." The detective was back on his feet. "Be smart, Drago, get on your horse and ride. Leave this area forever."

"How'd ya know my name?"

"I rode into Capstone right after you rawhided Lem. Sheriff Chandler told me all about it, gave me your description. I helped him look around town but you had left. Now I know where you went."

"Dehner, I'm gonna give ya the same chance ya gave—"

Drago hoped those words would cause Dehner to relax, if only for a moment. He drew his Colt and had started to fire when he felt an intense burn on his right leg and heard the shot from Dehner's gun. Drago jerked backwards, pressing the trigger of his gun which sent a shot sideways. The gunfighter struggled to stay on his feet and hold on to the gun which was now pointed toward the ground.

"Drop the gun!" Dehner shouted.

Drago looked upwards as if seeking divine guidance on what to do next. Blood spurted from his leg.

"Drop the gun!" Dehner shouted again.

A shot roared from directly behind Rance. With a fast backward glance, he spotted Rory Kagan holding a Remington, smoke coming from the barrel.

Rance quickly returned his eyes to George Drago. The gunfighter's body dropped to the earth. Dehner sensed immediately that Drago was dead, but he still ran toward the body. The detective was taking no chances. He scooped up the six shooter which had landed only inches from Drago's hand.

As he crouched over the gunfighter and pressed two fingers on his neck, feeling for a pulse that wasn't there, Dehner heard Lilly's footsteps running toward Rory Kagan. Dehner stood up and saw the couple embracing. The detective mused that, once again, a young man had killed an outlaw who might have provided valuable information. And, once again, there was no sense in bringing the matter up.

Rance stuck Drago's gun in his belt and

approached the couple. Lilly was examining Rory's head.

"No need to fuss," Rory said. "It ain't nothin' serious."

Dehner spoke in a calm neutral voice. "Are you okay, Miss Tantrall?"

"I'm fine, thank you, but Rory—"

Rance held up a palm and looked at the young man. "What happened tonight?"

Kagan pointed a thumb behind him, indicating the opposite side of the hill from where Lilly had come. "I tied up my horse in the trees back there and somethin' hit me from behind, hit me hard. The jasper you called Drago musta knocked me unconscious. When I woke up I could hear that snake jawin' . . . guess he was talkin' to you. I ran out in time to see him dancin' about with a gun in his hand."

"You're a good shot," Dehner said. "You hit him right in the middle of the chest."

Rory's eyes reflexively darted to Lilly. What he saw on her face made him feel good. "I know how to handle a gun."

"But you don't know how to take care of yourself." There was too much adoration in Lilly's voice for the criticism to be taken seriously. "You need to sit down." She guided Rory toward a knee-high boulder which squatted beside the cave and plunked him on it. "I'll be right back."

Rance watched Rory Kagan carefully as Lilly

retrieved cloths and a canteen from her saddle, then hurried into the cave to grab the candle. The young man seemed to be okay but then he could have been putting on a brave front for the young lady.

Lilly employed the candle light to get a good look at the cut on Rory's head. "The wound looks serious, your entire head is covered with blood." The light also revealed moistness in Lilly's eyes.

Dehner looked over Lilly's shoulder as he smiled and spoke softly, trying to calm the young woman. "The cut itself doesn't look deep. When you regained consciousness, Rory, did you run a hand over your head?"

"Can't recall . . . might have."

Rance lifted Kagan's right hand, placing it in the candle light, there were lines of blood on it. "You touched the wound, bloodied your hand, and then wiped it through your hair. Believe me; I've done that more than a few times myself."

A reassured Lilly began to clean and bandage the cut on Kagan's head. She paused for a moment to give Rance a suspicious look. "Mr. Dehner, what brought you to this location tonight?"

"You're lousy at deception, Miss Tantrall. I've been keeping as close an eye on you as I could. I saw you ride off tonight and followed you here."

The woman inhaled and for a moment looked away. "The deception is over. Tomorrow I'm telling Father everything."

"Guess I'll have to do the same," Kagan started to run a hand over his head once again, then stopped and settled for a long sigh. "Hate to think what Pa will do. Not to me so much but I know ma will take my side." Rory's voice rose in anger. "If that no good drunk hurts her, I swear, I'll kill him."

Lilly softly gripped the young man's shoulder. "I'll ask Father not to tell anyone—"

Rory inhaled and pressed his lips together in a determined manner. "No. I need to have a serious talk with Pa. I'd sure 'preciate you waiting a short spell before telling Elijah anything. Pa needs to hear it from me first."

"Of course, you're right." Lilly gently instructed Rory to hold the cloth against his wound and then began to speak about the hired killer. "Before he tried to . . . ah . . . attack me, Drago said that he almost killed Lem Donnigan this afternoon." She glanced at Dehner. "Did the sheriff tell you pretty much the same thing?"

The detective responded with a quick nod.

"That gunslick musta known today was Lem's day off and he usually spends it at the Wet Dog." Rory's voice trembled. "Pa will probably hire him another gunfighter . . . looks like the killing ain't gonna stop anytime soon."

"Don't be so pessimistic, Rory," the detective said.

The couple gave Dehner a questioning look.

He replied to their unspoken questions. "Those outlaws who have been attacking the homesteaders come from a lawless border town called Devil's Due. The place is run by a guy named Beau Rawlins. Rawlins is organizing the attacks."

The questioning look stayed on Lilly's face. "But . . . why?"

"Rawlins wants to move up in the world," Dehner answered. "He plans to start a war between the ranchers and homesteaders. Most of the small ranchers and homesteaders around here can't afford to hire gunfighters. They'll sell cheap in order to get out. Beau Rawlins will arrive with cash in hand. It's an old idea but it works more often than not."

Rory exchanged doubtful glances with Lilly before shifting his gaze back to Dehner. "This Rawlins fella must know a lot about this area."

The detective nodded his head. "There's a Judas operating in Capstone or somewhere nearby who is helping Rawlins: someone who knows where and when to attack."

Lilly now looked convinced. "That does make sense. Any idea who it is?"

Dehner pushed his hat back and scratched his head. "No, but whoever it is knows what he's doing. All of the attacks were well planned."

Rance looked at the young man. "I'm sure Rawlins sent George Drago to offer his services to your father. And he knew when your father would be open to such an offer."

Lilly squeezed Rory's shoulder. "This is awful. Mr. Dehner, you've got to find out who this person is or—"

"That may prove impossible," Dehner answered.

"Why?"

"I received a telegram today. The Texas Rangers are going to move in on Devil's Due and close it down. Maybe they won't be able to arrest Rawlins on any serious charges as they had hoped but they just don't believe Devil's Due can be allowed to continue."

Rory almost shouted. "But once Devil's Due is gone we might never find out who the traitor is!"

A look of resignation came over the detective. "I'm afraid that's right."

Lilly's thoughts were moving in a different direction. "You said the Rangers are going to 'move in,' Mr. Dehner. That sounds nice and neat but it won't be that way, will it? There's going to be more killing."

Rance kicked the ground. "I'll do everything I can, Miss Tantrall, to see to it that no more innocent people get killed."

Lilly didn't look reassured. Dehner couldn't blame her. The words sounded hollow and he knew it.

Chapter Sixteen

Beau Rawlins looked out his office window at the rising sun. He gave a mirthless laugh. Most Texans were getting up about now. For the residents of Devil's Due sunrise signaled a time of rest, or, at least, sleeping it off. On the floor below him a handful of desperate men were negotiating with whores to spend the daylight hours in bed with them. Unlike most of the jaspers in his town they couldn't be satisfied with collapsing into a drunken slumber. They had to have a woman beside them.

Rawlins laughed again, this time louder and harsher. "They call themselves hardcases but at bedtime, they're like children crying for mommy," he said aloud.

A tap on the door startled him. Did someone hear him talking to himself? He assumed his businessman's voice and pose. "Come in."

Gail entered cautiously, holding a cup and saucer. "I brought your coffee, Mr. Rawlins, jus' like you asked."

Beau's voice became friendly, "Thanks, put it on the desk."

As the woman followed instructions, Beau

ratcheted up the friendly tone, "Tell me, Gail, is that religious jasper giving you any more trouble?"

Gail appeared surprised by both the question and her boss's good natured approach. "No sir, Hosea is . . . he's no problem at all."

"Well, if he tries to hassle you again, jus' let me know."

"Yes, sir."

"And, you don't have to call me, sir. To you, I'm Beau."

"Yes sir . . . I mean, Beau."

Rawlins tried to look casual as he stepped toward his desk, picked up the coffee cup and took a sip. "There are some changes coming soon. And you are going to be a part of those changes."

Gail patted her hair nervously. "Yes . . . Beau . . . whatever you say."

Beau Rawlins fell silent for a moment. His eyes shifted to the coffee cup which he now held in his hand. "Have you heard . . . Polly is leaving?"

"I heard."

"I want you to take her place."

"But sir . . . Beau . . . I can't do that! I mean, the other girls, they won't take orders from me like they do from Polly."

"I'll see to it that they do!" Beau returned his coffee cup to the saucer on the desk. "I'm sure you'll want the job when you think over all the advantages." Rawlins carefully eyed his employee. Her face was pale and her smile forced.

"You'll feel good about the changes when you have time to think it over, Gail. Ah . . . you can leave now . . . we'll talk about this later."

"Yes sir." She turned and hastily left the office.

Rawlins stared at the closed door. Gail had been less than pleased with his offer. Hell, she looked terrified.

Beau collapsed into his office chair, and bowed his head into cupped hands. The last few hours had been a nightmare.

Rawlins had been working in his office, indifferent to the nightly ruckus going on beneath him. He pulled out the bottom drawer of his desk, only to find that the bottle there was nearly empty.

"I should check on the action downstairs anyway," the saloon owner said to himself. "I'll pick up a bottle while I'm down there."

Rawlins had just stepped out of the office when he heard Polly's unmistakable laughter trilling over the upstairs hallway. What was she doing upstairs? Polly was in charge of the girls. She wasn't supposed to be using the upstairs rooms herself. She was *his* woman.

Rawlins's office was tucked into a corner that made a U at the end of the hall and fronted the stairway. He was out of Polly's sight. He stood still and listened as Polly spoke.

"You've got a lot of money, cowboy," she purred. "I bet you worked hard for that cash."

"Yep, robbin' a bank is sure enough hard work."

Polly gave a harsh laugh and then continued. "I think you're gonna like Devil's Due. And, if you get bored, jus' come see Polly."

"I thought ya was keepin' company with the boss man."

"The boss man spends most his time cooped up in his office; he even eats there. Rawlins is plenty busy working the books and getting fat," Polly's voice went from playful to sensuous. "You and me can spend our time getting some . . . exercise."

The couple was laughing together as they went down the stairway. Neither one of them looked behind to see Beau Rawlins.

Rawlins watched the man with his arm around Polly. He was the kind of man Beau wanted to be and knew he wasn't: tall, broad shouldered, and muscular. The type of man other men would naturally respect and even fear.

Beau Rawlins felt puny and insignificant. He closed his eyes and squeezed his hands into fists. Opening his eyes he inhaled deeply and then walked quickly down the stairs. He owned this saloon and he owned this town. Maybe some people needed to be reminded of that.

Rawlins stopped at the bar and shouted at the apron. "Give me a bottle, you know what I like."

The barkeep was taking orders from two customers who had just arrived. "Sure, Boss, just a minute."

"Now!"

The barkeep looked both surprised and faintly scared. "Sure, Boss." He retrieved a bottle from under the counter and handed it to Rawlins.

Few people in the Fast Dollar had noticed the exchange. Rawlins looked around the saloon. Polly was standing at one of the poker tables. He would assert his authority once again and show the woman Beau Rawlins in action.

"Hello, Beau," Polly greeted the saloon owner as he approached the table.

Rawlins was shocked by the casualness of her words. The woman spoke as if everything between them was exactly the same. As if she hadn't just betrayed him with some two bit saddle bum. Beau's anguish grew more intense. For how long had Polly been cheating on him? How many people knew about it?

Rawlins felt an urgent need to assert his strength. He looked at Stacey Hooper who was sitting at the table studying his cards with the usual smug grin.

"There's something I want to say to you!" Rawlins shouted at the gambler.

Hooper didn't lift his eyes from his cards. "Go

ahead, Beau, you know how much I value your wisdom."

Beau fell silent for a moment. He couldn't think of anything to say. Finally he yelled out, "I want you to stop hanging around with that religious moron. Why does he preach in the streets anyway?"

Hooper gave Rawlins a quick glance. "You won't let him preach in the saloon, Beau."

There were a few guffaws from the table and Polly giggled a bit. "It ain't funny," Rawlins tried to sound strong and only sounded jittery. "That man is a trouble maker."

Stacey gave the saloon owner a benign look. "Beau, you're the one who named this town Devil's Due. Hosea Rimstead represents the side of the angels. Pitchforks versus harps. I think the odds are on your side, but then you can never tell. Angels do come up with some unexpected surprises."

More light laughter followed Stacey's remark. Rawlins felt frustrated and a bit foolish. He turned to Polly. "I need to see you in my office."

"What for?"

"I want to see you in my office—now!"

"OK, OK." The woman sounded irritated, not cowed.

As he walked up the stairway behind Polly, Beau tried to think of something to say, a way to express the hollowness and despair inside him.

There were no words for it. Polly had been the only sure thing in his life. She loved him and would always stand beside him; in a few horrible moments that assurance had been ripped from him and could never be replaced.

The couple entered Beau's office. Rawlins walked behind his desk and stood there facing the woman who had a bored smirk on her face. Suddenly, Beau realized how he could withstand the loss: hatred, the one emotion which had already allowed him to survive and defeat his enemies.

"You cheap tramp!" The words came out as a hiss.

"What are you talkin' about, Beau?"

"I saw you with that saddle bum. After all the advantages I've given you, you're still nothing but a lowly—"

"Let me tell you something, Beau Rawlins, that saddle bum was twice the man you are! You can have your so-called advantages. I'm sick of you, just like the next woman you try to buy will be!"

"You're finished in this town!"

"Oh, what a tragedy! I'm finished in this town . . . Beau Rawlins's town, a third rate dive. Yes, third rate jus' like the so-called man who runs it. I'll be riding out on my buckboard in the morning." The woman turned and made fast strides toward the door.

"I bought you that buckboard." Rawlins's words

were blurted out and sounded sad and desperate, the intense emotion of before momentarily gone.

Polly stopped in the open doorway and sneered at her former boss, "Thanks." She slammed the door behind her.

Beau Rawlins's head lurched upward as a knock sounded on the door. He cleared his throat to make sure his voice didn't sound broken. "Yes?"

"Toby Colton, Mr. Rawlins, the barkeep said you wanted to see me."

The saloon owner hastily ran his hands over his face, wiping away all signs of wetness. He scooted some papers from the corner of the desk to the center, making it appear he was working on them. "Come in."

Toby Colton ambled inside and closed the door. Colton was older than most of the residents of Devil's Due: somewhere in his mid-forties. He stood at average height with a worn, craggy face. Unlike George Drago, Colton wasn't particularly fast with a gun or intimidating. But there was a cold competence about Toby Colton and that's what Beau needed right now.

"Do you know Polly?" Rawlins asked.

"The Queen of the Fast Dollar, sure."

"I jus' kicked the queen off her damn throne. She's leaving town today. That tramp knows far too much. I want her killed but wait 'till she's a safe distance from Devil's Due."

Colton's face remained passive. "When's she leavin'?"

Rawlins gave a bitter laugh. "She said she was leaving in the morning. Hell, that tramp never pulls her body out of bed before nine. She'll probably ride out on that buckboard of hers sometime in the late morning but you'll have to keep an eye out."

"Sure." Befitting his personality, Colton's voice was a steady monotone. "Ya know, Mr. Rawlins, a job like this sounds simple but it can git complicated. I'd like to take some men with me. Call it insurance, if ya'd like."

"Handle it any way you want, Toby, jus' get the job done."

"Another thing, Polly ain't hard to look at, ain't hard at all, some jaspers will want to have a bit of fun, that OK?"

A wave of nausea engulfed Beau Rawlins. He clasped a hand over his mouth, blocking a surge of vomit. He looked down at the papers in front of him, pretending to have little interest in Toby's question. "Ah . . . I'll leave that to you, Colton; any more questions?"

"No sir."

"Let me know when the job's done, that's all for now."

The moment Colton was gone, Rawlins began breathing heavily. His hands shook and this time he leaned over the box of sand to throw up. He brushed sand over the vomit, then stood up and tried to walk off his dizziness.

"I'm going to be very rich . . . soon," he whispered to an empty room. "Gotta stay strong, gotta stay strong."

Rawlins slammed his right fist into his left palm. Could he continue without Polly? She was the one person he could confide in; even confided about his fears. She was the one person he could trust to always be loyal and . . .

A laugh of absolute despair shot from Beau's throat. "I can't trust anyone, nobody!"

Rawlins stepped over to the window to gaze out on Devil's Due. What he saw brought him no comfort. "That damned Judas, what's he doing here?!"

Beau inhaled and calmed himself. He still needed Judas to keep him informed about what was going on in Capstone. But the fact that he was back in Devil's Due now could only be bad news.

Rawlins settled back in behind his desk and once again pretended to be reading the papers in front of him. He listened as footsteps ran up the wooden stairs and answered with a "come in" to the hasty knocks on the office door.

"What are you doing here?" the saloon owner asked.

"I have important news," said Rory Kagan.

Chapter Seventeen

Rawlins was back on his feet, furiously working a cigar he had just lit after hearing Kagan's news. "Drago is dead and the Rangers are comin'. We gotta think this over careful. When do the Texas Rangers plan to hit Devil's Due?"

"Don't know."

"You don't know?!"

Rory yelled his reply. "I couldn't ask Dehner too many questions, he'd become suspicious!"

Kagan inhaled, paused and then spoke in a lowered voice. "Look, it'll be a few days before the Rangers get organized and make their way to Devil's Due. We got time left and we need to use it."

"Whatta you have in mind?"

An odd smile appeared on Rory Kagan's face and his eyes became unsettled. "Tomorrow, after sundown the night riders will strike again. This time, they're gonna kidnap Lilly Tantrall."

"You're loco," Rawlins snapped. "We can't attack the Tantrall ranch, too many men there who are loyal to Elijah. They'd fight us . . . fight us hard."

This time, Kagan's smile was one of smug

superiority. "No need to attack the ranch. I'm going to arrange a meeting with Lilly. The night riders will kidnap her while she is on her way and take her to an abandoned shack. I'll rescue her. The kidnappers will escape but before they do, they'll have told Lilly that Glenn Kagan is behind the abduction and all the destruction and killings."

An ash dropped from Beau's cigar and exploded on the office's thin carpet. Rawlins didn't seem to mind. "That would do it," his voice resounded with approval. "Tantrall would hit your father with a vengeance. There would be an all out war."

"But a short war," the fidgety look returned to Kagan's eyes. "My father will hire a few gunnies but he can't afford much. The other sodbusters will talk tough but fold real easy. Even a few of the small ranchers will vamoose. They don't have the guts for a real fight."

"I'll scoot Devil's Due tomorrow and leave the saddle bums for the Rangers." Rawlins laughed contentedly. "I'll set up shop in Capstone and start buying land."

"And when all that is over, you'll turn over a nice chunk of that land to me; you're nothing without me—"

"Sure Rory, I'm right grateful for all you've done. Tell me, whatta you gonna do with all that land?"

"I'm gonna start my own cattle ranch, be as big as Elijah, maybe bigger. And I'm gonna marry Lilly Tantrall." Rory's voice changed, it became more wistful and distant. He seemed to be talking to himself. "Poor Glenn Kagan, he might get killed or he might end up in jail. Even better, he could spend the rest of his life a nobody while his son is one of the most important men in town and married to the daughter of a man he hates!"

Rawlins once again realized he would never understand Rory Kagan. Like him, the kid wanted money and power but he wanted it all for such an odd reason. For Kagan, the most important thing was to defeat and humiliate his father. Beau couldn't understand such motives and felt confirmed in his plans to kill Rory Kagan once the kid was no longer needed.

"You better put your best men on this!"

Rory's command had interrupted his partner's thoughts. "Wha—"

"I've drawn you a map of the trail Lilly will be riding tomorrow night." Kagan pulled a piece of paper from his side pocket. "Your gunslicks are to grab her and take her to the shack I have marked on the map. Once they get there, they will let her know that Glenn Kagan is behind everything. I'll barge in, gun in hand and they'll run. Make sure you've got good men on this, not a stupid hardcase like Drago, who—"

"You already tole me 'bout Drago getting

hisself ventilated. OK, the guy wasn't too smart."

"So, who have you got in mind?"

"I'll put Toby Colton on it—we can trust him."

That Toby Colton was able to blend into his surroundings was a testimony to his wily skills as an outlaw. At mid-morning the main street of Devil's Due was almost deserted; most of the town's citizens were asleep. Toby sat in a dilapidated chair that fronted the small Good Times saloon and pretended to snooze.

Colton was a patient man which partially accounted for his longevity in a dangerous profession. He was also an outlaw who had developed strong instincts for trouble. Beau Rawlins had obviously adored Polly, now he wanted her killed. This situation was more complicated than Rawlins had let on and Colton knew he had to be cautious, which is why he had hired three men to help him. Those men were now playing cards at a table deep inside the Good Times.

Across from the saloon was one of the town's two hotels. A large window fronted the lobby and Toby had been making good use of it. About a half hour back that fancy dressed gambler, Stacey Hooper, had appeared in the lobby and remained there. Colton guessed that Hooper wanted to meet someone . . . and Polly stayed in that hotel.

Toby remained still with his hat pulled down

almost to his eyes as his theory was confirmed. Polly stepped into the lobby and Hooper
approached her. They exited the hotel together.
Colton could pick up a few of the gambler's
words.

"I'll be happy to ready your buckboard while
we discuss certain matters. You see, I want to
ensure you have a safe journey to Capstone."

Colton lackadaisically lifted himself from the
chair. Neither Stacey nor Polly noticed when he
began to follow them.

Chapter Eighteen

Colton and his three henchmen rode slowly up a small hill. They had been riding at a cautious pace in the hot weather, trying not to tire the animals too much. The most important work still lay ahead.

Toby eyed the two medium sized boulders near the foot of the knoll. The stones could provide cover for men but not horses.

"We'll wait for the buckboard here," Colton spoke as he guided the makeshift crew behind an irregular line of scrawny trees which topped the hill. "Not much cover, but it'll do. We're a far piece from Devil's Due. When she gets here, Polly will be relaxin' some."

"The boss man says he wants her killed a far ways from Devil's Due. You've sure pleasured him on that count." The remark came from an outlaw called Scar. A glance at the right side of his face revealed the source of his nickname.

"Yep, and we had to git us away from Devil's Due to find even a little hill." Colton swept an arm over their surroundings. "This ain't much but it'll make our job easier."

"That's the kinda job I likes, easy . . . and fun," Scar said.

The other henchmen laughed along with Scar and Colton pretended he also was enjoying himself. A life lived on the wrong side of the law had left Toby Colton with no illusions about the intelligence of outlaws. He pegged Scar as the best of the tacky threesome and the one most able to carry out orders. He had even forgotten the name of the other two, not that names meant anything when dealing with the residents of Devil's Due.

Colton pulled field glasses from one of his saddle bags and periodically checked the road below. After about twenty minutes he spotted a boil of dust moving toward Capstone.

"Gents, I do believe our lady is 'bout to arrive."

The three outlaws laughed in a lusty manner and made crude remarks as Colton knew they would. With an artificial smile spread across his face, Toby pointed to the two outlaws who were on the left side of Scar.

"The moment the wagon gits even with the hill, you two ride down and stop it, then Scar and I will join you."

One of the men he had pointed at looked confused. "What fer? Be lots better if we all rode down at once."

"Scar and me will hold back, jus' in case," Toby broadened the smile. "And when it comes to welcoming the lady it'll be first come, first serve."

That was all the persuasion the two owlhoots needed. Colton hadn't bothered to tell the henchmen about the talk he had overheard between Polly and Stacey Hooper.

As his accomplices galloped down the hill toward the wagon, Scar began to gripe. "It ain't right, them two—"

"Shut up!" The smile was gone from Colton's face, replaced by a harsh intensity. Scar fell silent.

Colton watched through his field glasses as the two outlaws rode toward the wagon firing their guns into the air. Polly stopped the buckboard as the two men pulled up beside her, holstering their weapons.

Toby laughed contemptuously and whispered to himself. "Those fools didn't even spread out. They're both right close to the bed of the wagon, talkin' to the gal."

Colton closely watched that wagon bed which was covered by a large canvas tarp. There were a few bulges in the covering where Polly's bags were situated. But Colton knew bags weren't the only things the tarp hid.

The canvas was suddenly pushed back, revealing two men. Toby wasn't surprised to see Stacey Hooper, gun in hand, but a second gent carrying iron surprised him. "That's Hosea . . . whatshisname . . . the preacher man," he said aloud.

Scar gave his companion a confused look. "What in—"

"I tole ya to shut up . . . just do what I say."

Both men watched from the hill, Scar without field glasses. They could hear Stacey shout something, then shots followed. Polly screamed as both of the outlaws who had stopped her plunged from their mounts.

Panicked neighing and the hoof beats of two horses galloping off filled the air. Stacey and Hosea, guns in hand, jumped off the wagon and approached the two bodies that lay on the ground. As they crouched over the outlaws, Stacey holstered his gun while Hosea began to slowly reload his Winchester.

"Things is workin' out jus' fine." This time Colton's smile was genuine as he spoke to Scar.

"Jus' fine! Hell, looks like both of our guys jus' got kilt!"

"Yep," Toby snapped as he returned the field glasses to a saddle bag. "Now, you 'n' me is gonna do some killin'."

Scar followed Colton's lead as both men galloped down the hill firing at the two men who stood beside the corpses, guns holstered. Scar saw that both the men and Polly looked shocked and scared. *Looks like Colton had himself a good plan,* Scar thought. He was already looking forward to the fun that would follow the killing.

Chapter Nineteen

Rance Dehner wasn't surprised to see he was being followed. The detective reined up his bay and braced for trouble. Talking with a broken hearted young woman of nineteen would not be pleasant.

Lilly Tantrall pulled her palomino up and halted beside Rance. "Thank you for waiting for me, Mr. Dehner. I saw you leaving our ranch and, it may be wrong, but I have to talk with you."

The detective noted the arch formality in the young woman's voice. "You're welcome, Miss Tantrall, and, of course, I'll be happy to answer any questions."

"I think you are heading for that town you told me and Rory about last night, Devil's Due."

"That's correct, Miss Tantrall."

"You expect to find Rory there."

"Yes."

"You're wrong! Rory isn't a Judas! I knew you were getting insane ideas about Rory when you asked me all those questions this morning."

Dehner ignored the passion in Lilly's voice and spoke in a calm monotone. "I originally had questions for Rory. But when I got to the Kagan place he wasn't there. His mother told me he occasionally rides off for a day or two."

"He has to! Rory has to get away from that terrible father of his!"

"Maybe so."

"Rory is the finest man on God's earth, you don't understand him, he . . ."

Lilly's face began to contort and she looked away from the detective. Dehner wanted to say something comforting. He wanted to tell Lilly she was young, beautiful with a wonderful life ahead of her. A broken heart naturally accompanied youth. But the woman didn't want to hear that, not at the moment.

Somewhere, deep inside her, Lilly now realized Rory Kagan was scheming to create a land war. But she wasn't quite ready to let that knowledge surface. Rance decided to gently but firmly appeal to the woman's reason.

"Miss Tantrall, I was always suspicious of Rory."

"Why?"

"I had to be. Max Thompson was killed close to the cave where you and Rory would meet. We know the sheriff would patrol at night trying to locate the night riders; my guess runs that Max spotted you or Rory and decided to follow. But Rory saw him. Rory knew the area well, it wouldn't have been hard for him to sneak up on Max, take the sheriff downhill, kill him and then return to the cave pretending he had just arrived. Afterwards, he could have dumped the body in your barn."

"I might have done that! Why aren't you suspicious of me?" Lilly's voice collapsed into a sob. Her palomino nickered and shook its head as if trying to offer solace. The young woman patted the horse's neck, inhaled and collected her emotions. "I'm sorry."

"There's nothing to be sorry about, I understand." Dehner admitted to himself that he really didn't understand. He had always found Rory Kagan to be a bit creepy and wondered why his client's daughter didn't feel the same way. Did Rory's injury and troubled childhood touch Lilly's deep well of sympathy—a sympathy she mistook for love? Dehner immediately decided that such questions were beyond his ken.

When Lilly spoke again, it was almost in a whisper. "What else has made you suspicious of Rory?"

"Well, I'll have to confess, Miss Tantrall, I haven't always been open with you. Before the town meeting, I saw you and Rory giving each other signals. After the meeting, I followed you."

The light tone in Rance's voice did seem to change the young woman's mood a little bit. A wistful smile came to her face but it was a smile of sadness and loss.

The detective continued, "I stood outside the

cave and listened while you two talked. Rory hates his father. Hate is a powerful emotion."

"So is love."

Dehner let that pass. "Think back, carefully, Miss Tantrall, to the second time when I eavesdropped on you two. Rory was supposedly knocked out by George Drago near the cave where you met. Be honest with yourself, Miss Tantrall. The injury on Rory's head was little more than a slight cut. Drago probably gave Rory a tap on the head to break the skin. After that, Rory ran his hand through his hair to make it look like a serious injury."

"But Rory killed George Drago!"

"He saw that his plan had failed," Dehner replied. "Who knows what Drago might have spilled if he had lived? Rory couldn't let that happen."

Lilly's face went pale. She stroked the neck of her palomino as if the steed were the only thing she could depend on. "Rory knew Drago was going to—"

Dehner cut in quickly. "I think Rory had plotted a scheme with George Drago in advance. Rory would run into the cave in time to rescue you and be the hero. He would run Drago off but everyone would learn that a gunman hired by Glenn Kagan had attempted to . . . assault you. You are thought of very highly in Capstone, Miss Tantrall. There would have been a land war for sure. But when Rory approached the cave for his big entrance he saw me making my way to the front of the cave. There had to be a last minute change in the script."

The young woman began to cry. Rance could only hope he was right. After all, if Drago had actually violated Lilly Tantrall a very bitter land war would have ignited. That idea may have appealed to Rory Kagan, who was a hard man to understand.

Lilly pulled a handkerchief from a side pocket and began to dab at her eyes. "I'm sorry, Mr. Dehner. You must be getting tired of hearing me say that."

Rance was encouraged by the young woman's attempt at brave humor. He tried to move the conversation in another direction. "There's another thing that made me suspicious of Rory . . . a small thing . . . but last night Rory said that Drago must have known that Monday was Lem Donnigan's day off."

"So?"

"It's not likely that Glenn Kagan would know what day Lem had off or that Lem usually spent that day in the Wet Dog Saloon."

"I still don't follow you." The woman returned the handkerchief to her pocket.

"Lilly, at one time or another, you probably told Rory what day Lem had off and even where he spent it; that would be important information for a couple who were meeting secretly. After all, Lem is very loyal to your father. If he found out about the clandestine meetings . . ."

The young woman pressed her lips together and nodded her head.

"After Rory made the remark about Lem's day off, I told both of you a lie."

Lilly's face reflected surprise and confusion. Dehner responded. "I said that the Texas Rangers planned to invade Devil's Due and shut it down. That's not true, but Rory bought it. I'm sure he is in Devil's Due right now warning Beau Rawlins and proving he's the Judas we've been after."

Lilly didn't respond to Dehner's last statement. "So, the Rangers are still looking for a way to get evidence against this Beau Rawlins. They want to arrest and convict him?"

"Right, and—"

Shots sounded in the distance. Dehner stood up in his stirrups. "I can't see much but those shots seem to be coming from a hill up ahead."

"Rory could be involved!" the woman shouted.

"Go back home, Miss Tantrall!" Dehner spurred his bay into a gallop.

Lilly had no intention of obeying the order. She remained where she was for several minutes. Then she followed behind the detective at a steady lope.

Chapter Twenty

As the detective approached the hill, he could see two men positioned behind boulders. They were firing at a buckboard. Dehner could tell there was one person lying in the bed of the wagon and at least one person under it.

He turned his horse off the trail and rode behind the knoll before anyone could spot him. He was in view but, from what the detective could tell, all parties involved were too busy firing at each other to pay him any notice.

Behind the hill, Dehner tethered his horse to the ground, yanked field glasses from his saddle bags, looped the strap around his neck, and started up the knoll. At the top, he quickly lay on the browned grass and put the glasses to his eyes.

The man in the buckboard was Stacey Hooper! The gambler was using the wagon's wooden side as a shield. He was rolling about desperately as explosions of wood fragments made by piercing bullets peppered him.

Dehner needed to act immediately. He silently cursed himself for leaving his Winchester in its saddle boot but couldn't take the time to retrieve it. Stacey's fortress was becoming increasingly vulnerable and the detective wondered how much ammunition his friend had left.

Rance left the field glasses on the hilltop and advanced downward, Colt in hand. Both gunmen had their horses secured to the ground by rocks. Those horses gave loud whinnies as Dehner drew near but the mounts had already been making plenty of noise in response to the shooting. Dehner gave a loud yell, "Drop the guns—now!"

Colton and Scar did what they were told. They arose from their crouches and faced the detective as he moved toward them. Dehner kept a close eye on the gunmen but not on their steeds. As he passed behind a roan, the panicked animal kicked up a back foot and hit Dehner in the shoulder, knocking him sideways and onto the ground.

Now it was Rance's turn to do a fast roll in order to save his life. A bullet from a retrieved gun struck a nearby rock, ricocheted to the ground and caused dust to spray against Dehner's leg. Without taking time to aim or even to look carefully at his adversaries Dehner fired from his position on the ground.

His shot missed but was close enough. "Let's get outta here!" a voice cried out.

Dehner fired another shot as he struggled onto his feet. But he was off balance and some plant debris now embedded in one eye blurred his vision. The bullet whined harmlessly through the air as the two gunmen buoyed onto their saddles and spurred their steeds. A couple of shots came from the buckboard but failed to find their marks.

The detective breathed deeply a few times. He blinked away the debris and his sight began to clear. From the other side of the road he could see Stacey Hooper standing in the buckboard, shouting at him as he gestured frantically. "Rance, stop those men! Don't let them get back to Devil's Due."

"OK!" Dehner was still a bit short of breath but Stacey appeared to have heard him.

The detective did the closest thing he could to running over the hill and back to his bay. He took one more deep breath before mounting and riding off after the two outlaws. As his horse again broke into a gallop it occurred to Dehner that he didn't know why Stacey thought it important to keep the outlaws from returning to Devil's Due, but he was willing to take the gambler's word on it.

The flat land made it possible for Rance to quickly bring his targets into sight. What started as two distant specks became two distinct riders; one was several strides in front of the other. Dehner's bay stretched his body out, the gelding's hoofs quickly and gracefully flying over the ground as he gained on the two riders.

The detective could now see that the gap between the two outlaws was becoming larger. The faster rider was several feet in front of his partner. Taking down both men would be a hard task.

The outlaw closest to Dehner pulled his six gun and fired at the oncoming detective. Dehner did not respond in kind. Bullets fired from a galloping horse rarely posed a threat. Rance needed to gain more ground before using his Colt.

The detective saw the front rider also draw his gun. What happened next shocked Dehner. The front rider fired a bullet into his partner's horse. A painful wail rose over the flat, dismal land as the animal collapsed to the ground, throwing its rider to the side of the road.

Dehner pulled up, dismounted and calmed his own steed who had been terrified by the horror in front of him. He didn't want the bay to go any closer to the wounded horse as the smell of blood could disturb the animal even more. He walked the bay off the road and secured his reins to the ground with a heavy stone.

About twenty yards ahead of him, the wounded horse thrashed in the dust and screeched in pain. Dehner watched as the thrown rider got to his feet, drew his gun, and began to run. A limp slowed his progress. The outlaw looked about desperately for a tree or boulder where he could fend off a pursuer but could spot nothing.

"Stop!" Dehner yelled as the owlhoot continued to run. The detective gave it another try. "You're injured; you haven't got a chance, give up!"

Rance muttered a curse and, Colt in hand, pursued his prey. The limping outlaw could not move fast and Rance quickly gained on him. Dehner saw the outlaw turn. The detective unleashed two bullets into his adversary, who stumbled and dropped his gun before his body dropped onto it.

Dehner ran to the fallen outlaw, who was struggling to sit up and grab the gun which now lay under his back. "I'll get that for you, friend," Rance's voice dripped with sarcasm as he yanked the weapon from behind his opponent. He felt a slight touch of sympathy for the outlaw, whose face melted in defeat as his body returned to the ground.

"What's your name?" the detective asked.

"Name's Sid, people call me Scar . . . guess why."

Dehner crouched beside Sid. "Why were you and your partner firing at that wagon?"

"Colton, the snake who shot my horse, says we wuz killin' Polly for Beau Rawlins."

"Why?"

Sid's voice became faint. "Don't know . . . don't care . . . get me a doc . . ." The man who everyone called Scar mumbled a few stray curses before falling permanently silent.

Dehner stood up and stuck Sid's gun in his belt. The other hired killer, the one Sid had called Colton, was now too far ahead for the detective to catch up with him. Dehner realized that's why Colton had shot his partner's horse. A confrontation between Sid and the man chasing after them would give Colton plenty of time to make a clean break.

Dehner heard wails coming from the road that were becoming increasingly faint. He knew what he had to do.

As the detective approached the wounded animal, he realized that the roan was the mount who had given him a kick in the shoulder. The pain was already subsiding, Dehner had been lucky. The kick had only brushed him and not been a direct hit.

Rance looked the strawberry roan over carefully, confirming his worst fears. The animal had broken a leg in the fall.

Dehner got down on one knee and began to gently pet the horse's side. The roan was breathing deeply and its eyes were flared.

"This isn't anything personal, fella. I should have had enough sense not to walk behind a scared horse. You just weren't very lucky, and fell in with bad company."

Rance gave the horse a final pat, then stood up. He didn't want to look the roan in the eye but knew he had no choice. Dehner took the gun belonging to Sid and fired a bullet into the animal's brain.

The detective hurried back to his own horse.

He needed to get back to Stacey and whoever was with him, and find out what was going on. Dehner didn't look back as he rode off. He realized he was leaving behind two bodies for the vultures and coyotes; one was a horse, the other was a man named Sid.

He felt a lot worse about the horse than he did about the man.

Chapter Twenty-One

Dehner laughed inwardly as he rode up to the buckboard. Lilly Tantrall was there. He had never really believed she would obey his instructions to return home. The young woman had just dismounted from her palomino; behind her were two more saddled horses. Dehner could hear her speaking to Stacey Hooper who was in the bed of the buckboard along with Hosea Rimstead.

"I had no trouble finding the horses. They both seem to be just fine." Obviously, the young woman had approached the wagon, introduced herself and offered to help.

"Thank you very much, Miss Lilly," Stacey replied gallantly. "You are being an invaluable help to us in this hour of crisis." The gambler turned and spoke to Rance as he rode up.

"Ah, good friend, I hope you, like Miss Lilly, have succeeded in your mission."

"Only half succeeded, Stacey. One of those outlaws is dead but the other is still on his way to Devil's Due."

"Your failure does make our predicament more perilous and urgent." Stacey jumped off the wagon and Hosea Rimstead followed behind him.

Dehner noticed two long bulges in the tarp that still covered the bed of the wagon. Stacey appeared pleased by his friend's attention to detail. "Our wagon was attacked by ruffians from Devil's Due. Hosea and I managed to dispatch two of them to Hades. The bodies of the dead men are now in the buckboard. They will be taken to where they can be given a decent burial. The west is becoming civilized, Rance, propriety must be observed."

"The two horses the young lady just rode up with, they must have belonged to the dead outlaws."

"Indeed. Hosea and I will be requiring their use. Your failure has placed us in a most awkward situation."

"Stacey, why don't you fill me in on what's been going on?"

As he faced the gambler directly, Dehner had been watching Lilly from the corner of his eye. The young woman had been trying to talk with a woman the detective recognized as Polly from the Fast Dollar Saloon. They were standing beside the wagon's horses. Polly was only a few years older than the rancher's daughter but she still seemed to feel ill at ease in her presence. Lilly was having to work at keeping any conversation alive.

"Happy to bring you up to date," Stacey declared as he looked towards Polly. "I'm sure you recognize Polly, the Queen of the Fast Dollar."

"Yes," Dehner now looked directly at the former saloon girl as he nodded and touched his hat.

"Polly was exiled from Devil's Due by Beau in one of his irrational fits of bad temper," Stacey continued. "That news spread around town fast; the citizens, predominantly male, disagreed strongly with Beau's move."

Stacey had intended his last remark as a compliment. He smiled graciously at Polly but the woman didn't respond. Her face remained passive. Standing beside Stacey was Hosea Rimstead, who looked fidgety. Dehner reckoned that Hosea, being in love with a saloon girl himself, would find the topic of Polly's dismissal a bit unnerving.

Stacey Hooper seemed oblivious to the discomfort he was causing. He continued in his jovial manner. "Fortunately, I have had past dealings with Beau and realized he would consider it necessary to permanently silence Polly. Therefore, I came up with the excellent scheme of having Hosea and myself hide under a tarp in Polly's buckboard and thus be available when the inevitable attack on her life came."

Hosea's face crunched in doubt. "But you sure didn't reckon on four attackers! Once we brought down those first two jaspers, I thought it was done . . . so did you, Stacey."

"A minor oversight," the gambler's mood remained chipper. "When those other two villains came galloping down the hill on their steeds, we were able to drive them behind the boulders with only a little fuss."

Rimstead remained dubious. "Took a lot of fuss if you ask me! You had to jump in the wagon and I had to crawl under it with Miss Polly. We was runnin' out of ammo when Rance came along. He was a real answer to prayer."

Stacey waved his hand as if repelling a pesky insect. "If Rance had not appeared I'm sure the Divine could have used us to fulfill his purpose. In fact, we probably would have prevented any of those ruffians from getting to Devil's Due."

Dehner reinserted himself into the discussion. "Why was it so important to keep all of the outlaws from returning to Devil's Due?"

"I would have thought a detective could figure out that angle on his own." Hooper's voice became resigned, a man having to suffer fools. "You see, Beau was in no way discreet when it came to his conversations with Polly. He told her everything about his nefarious schemes. Rawlins will soon know that Polly is alive and able to testify against him. He will vacate the town he built and go who knows where. Polly's life will continue to be in danger and I will have failed in my mission for the Texas Rangers."

The gambler's words caused Dehner to pause

for an odd reason. Stacey had called Rawlins's former mistress "Polly" while Hosea had referred to her as "Miss Polly."

Of course, most saloon girls only go by a first name and often that name is phony. And the demand of courtesy that gentlemen first request a lady's permission before using her first name had never applied to saloon girls, many of whom were also prostitutes. In all likelihood neither Stacey nor Hosea knew Polly's last name. But Hosea, going by his own decent instincts, had demonstrated respect for the woman by calling her, "Miss Polly." The more sophisticated Stacey Hooper had lower standards. Rance had to admit to himself that, like Stacey, he would naturally have called Rawlins's mistress Polly. Maybe he needed to listen more carefully to Hosea's preaching and follow his example.

Hooper's voice shattered Dehner's thoughts. "You look deep in thought, my friend. Perhaps you are coming up with a plan to atone for your earlier sin!"

The detective thought it best not to mention his real thoughts and jerked himself back into the current predicament. "Rawlins believes the Texas Rangers are about to invade Devil's Due."

Hosea's face crunched again. "Why?"

"No time to explain," Dehner answered. "We need to get to Devil's Due, arrest Beau Rawlins now that we have a witness who will testify against him, and take him to Capstone. He can sit in jail there until the Rangers decide what to charge him with and where to hold the trial."

"An elementary but practical suggestion," Stacey declared. "We must leave at once."

"What 'bout Miss Polly?"

Again, Dehner noticed Hosea's reference to "Miss Polly" but he took no time to reflect on it. He nodded at the horses belonging to the two dead outlaws. "There are rifles in the scabbards of both those saddles. Why don't you two gents check out the nags while I talk with the ladies. I think we can get Miss Polly to safety soon."

As Rance approached the two ladies, he noticed a look of firm determination on Lilly's face. No doubt, she had been half listening to his conversation with Stacey and Hosea while she was talking with the former saloon girl.

"Mr. Dehner, I'm coming with you to Devil's Due. I have to talk with Rory, hear his side of—"

Polly's eyes widened as her entire face suddenly seemed vibrant with energy. "Do you mean, Rory Kagan?"

The saloon girl's sudden shout stunned Lilly. "Ah . . . yes."

"You're that Lilly!" The saloon girl's voice became even more forceful, "Lilly Tantrall, the daughter of the rancher."

"Yes."

"Honey, you're beautiful and rich, how'd you

ever get mixed up with a no good like Rory Kagan?"

To Dehner's surprise Lilly didn't appear angered by Polly's statement; instead she looked sheepish as she fumbled for words. "A lot of people misunderstand Rory—"

Polly gave a harsh laugh. "Misunderstand my . . . foot!" She saw the hurt look on Lilly Tantrall's face and softened her voice. "Honey, I've heard Rory Kagan when he was jawin' with Beau Rawlins. Men are like that when it comes to women, well, women like me, they sometimes talk like we're not there."

"Yes," Lilly said, "I understand."

"That boyfriend of yours is in cahoots with Rawlins. They're gonna start a land war, so they can move in and buy up farms and ranches cheap."

Lilly began to work her hands. "I just can't believe Rory is doing all these things."

The former saloon girl paused as if giving some thought to whether she should make the next statement. Determination suddenly shot into her eyes and she plowed forward. "Do you know what Rory Kagan finds most attractive about you?"

Lilly shrugged her shoulders.

"You're Elijah Tantrall's daughter. Glenn Kagen hates Elijah and Rory hates his papa. Marryin' you is jus' a small part of Rory's plans to make dear old dad poor and miserable."

Lilly looked at the ground and whispered words no one could decipher. Polly reached over and touched her arm. "I'm sorry, honey, but—"

Lilly's voice became firm and clear. "Don't be sorry, you told the truth, no one should ever be sorry about that."

Dehner jumped at the chance to cut in. "Miss Polly is going to be telling the truth about Beau Rawlins and Rory Kagan to the law, but she needs your help, Miss Tantrall."

Surprise and confusion wiped the other emotions from Lilly's face. "What do you mean?"

"We need to keep Miss Polly safe," Dehner explained. "Right now, we are about five hours from the Tantrall Ranch. I want you to take Miss Polly there." The detective gave a quiet, sardonic laugh. "Your father will have to find someplace to bury those buzzards in the wagon bed but there is a job a lot more important than that."

Dehner looked directly at the former saloon girl. "I want you to tell Elijah Tantrall everything you know about Devil's Due and Rawlins's schemes to start a land war, including his partnership with Rory Kagan."

Polly nodded her head, "Sure."

The detective's gaze shifted to the younger woman. "Miss Tantrall, tell your father that I and, ah, two friends are riding into Devil's Due to arrest Beau Rawlins. Elijah is to make his ranch a fortress. If we fail, there could be another attempt on Miss Polly's life. She must be kept safe."

"She will be!" the rancher's daughter declared before speaking directly to Polly. "We have a foreman, Lem Donnigan, who will make sure that no one comes near you who shouldn't, I promise!"

Dehner was pleased and a bit relieved by the determination in the young woman's voice. Lilly Tantrall now had an important duty which demanded she keep her emotional trauma in a tight compartment. Dehner watched Lilly tie her palomino to the back of the buckboard and then join Polly on the spring seat.

"Rory Kagan is a fool," Rance whispered to himself as he trotted to his bay, yanked a Winchester from the scabbard of his saddle and then quickly walked back to the wagon and handed Lilly the rifle.

"I don't think you'll need that, but you have it just in case." The detective gave the sky a fast glance. "There's several hours of sunlight left, you should get to the ranch before it gets too dark."

"You don't know how I drive a buckboard, mister," Polly spoke playfully as she nodded her head at Lilly. "I'll have this girl home in time for supper!"

Both women were laughing as the wagon pulled away. Dehner returned to his horse where Stacey and Hosea were already on their steeds and ready to ride.

Hosea Rimstead spoke as the detective mounted. "Gents, we need to take a moment for prayer before we go into battle—"

"I appreciate the thought, Hosea," Stacey interrupted. "But we really want to get to Devil's Due as fast as—"

Hosea continued, ". . . seein' as we are goin' up against a whole town of killers."

Stacey's eyebrows shot up. "Yes, the odds are somewhat against us. I suppose taking a moment to petition the Divine for any help he may wish to render would not be out of order. Please excuse my earlier impatience, Hosea and present our case to the heavens."

Hosea presented their case and then the three men rode for Devil's Due.

Chapter Twenty-Two

The sun shone at eye level as the odd threesome approached Devil's Due. "This is downright strange," Dehner spoke as he eyed the town slowly coming into view. "I don't hear sounds of any activity at all."

Hosea Rimstead was riding between the detective and the gambler. "Devil's Due is a den of sin. Those jaspers are like the ones the Good Book talks about. They want nothin' to do with light. Darkness is what they're after. Most of the town is still sleepin' or jus comin' awake."

"Making this the ideal time for our little charade!" Stacey announced in a stage whisper. "I have observed how the town operates in the daytime. There are four men who patrol the town. Two stand duty on the north end of Devil's Due, where we will be entering. Those gents are our immediate concern."

Stacey held a hand up, indicating that the procession needed to halt. "Can't take any chances; soon we will be within range of field glasses. As they say in the theater, 'places, everyone.'"

Hosea pulled back and yanked a Winchester from the boot of his saddle. Rance and Stacey wrapped ropes around their wrists and kept their hands on the horns of their saddles to make it appear that the hands were bound.

Hosea spoke to his companions as the threesome continued to ride toward Devil's Due. "Mighty grateful to you gents for helpin' me get Gail outta that den of iniquity and makin' it our first stop. She might need some persuadin' but she wants to be my woman, I know it. The good Lord has ordained that we should be together."

"Ah, Hosea!" Stacey began to lift an arm as he spoke but quickly checked himself. "That is where you have gone wrong. You should be appealing to the lady's heart; save your theological observations for another time."

As the gambler continued to pontificate on the mysterious depths of a woman's heart, an odd undercurrent ran through Dehner's thoughts. Why was Stacey Hooper giving such priority to the romantic travails of Hosea and Gail? The gambler seemed to genuinely like the couple. He wanted things to work out well for them. Perhaps Stacey saw something in the relationship between Hosea and Gail that reminded him of a long ago loss.

Dehner sighed. Stacey Hooper had certainly picked the worst time to be a nursemaid to the lovelorn.

The threesome became quiet as they drew near Devil's Due. Waves of late afternoon heat zig-zagged crazily in front of them like ghosts guarding a portal to the netherworld. At the edge of the town was a house which Dehner reckoned belonged to Beau Rawlins. Who else would own a house in a place like Devil's Due? Beside the house was the town's livery. There could be quite a few reasons why Rawlins wanted the livery close by.

As the riders passed the livery, two of Beau's henchmen, both holding rifles, stepped off the boardwalk that fronted a small saloon. One of them set down a bottle that they had been sharing. They stared at the strange horsemen that approached.

"It's that crazy preacher man, Lou."

"Yeah, and he's got that gambler fella with him; don't know who the other jasper is." Both gunmen were tall, with large foreheads and deep set eyes. Not surprising. Lou and Sherm Proctor were brothers who spent half of their lives stealing and the other half in Devil's Due.

Sherm carefully eyed the horsemen. "That's the fella who outdrew Lars Olsen. Watch him real careful. I'll stand on their right side, you take the left."

Lou nodded as he raised his rifle and yelled, "Stop right there!"

"Howdy, gents!" Hosea sounded upbeat and confident. "I got me two prisoners that mister Rawlins will wanna see."

Sherm didn't raise his rifle, but there was suspicion in his voice. "Whadda you talkin' 'bout, Sky Pilot?"

Hosea pointed his rifle at the two riders in front of him. "I useta think these two were fine Christian gentlemen. Then last night I caught 'em stealin' from the cash box at the Fast Dollar. Guess I've been hangin' out in bad company. I owe Mr. Rawlins an apology."

Sherm's suspicion diminished but it was still there. "Nobody told me 'bout money bein' taken from the Fast Dollar."

Hosea shrugged his shoulders. "Well, that's what happened. Got the loot in my saddle bags. Come see."

Both brothers lowered their rifles and stepped toward Hosea's saddle. Rance jumped Sherm while Stacey pounced on Lou. Both outlaws were knocked unconscious. Their bodies were dragged behind the saloon where they were bound and gagged.

Hosea looked down at the two outlaws, both regaining consciousness but too weak to try to break out of the ropes. "Let this be a lesson to both you gents. Lust for filthy lucre always leads to a downfall."

"We'll have to end the sermon there." Dehner looked about and listened carefully. "We'll move down the back way to the Fast Dollar."

They tethered their horses behind the small

saloon and made their way down the row of wooden structures. Dehner tried to recall the exact set up of the town. Besides Rawlins's house and the livery there were seven buildings. Four of them were saloons. There was a gun shop which doubled as a general store and two Hotels with restaurants which housed most of the town's population.

They stopped at the back door of the Fast Dollar. Rance tried the door, which was locked. The detective pointed to a nearby window. "Breaking the glass will probably make less noise than busting down the door."

Rance pulled his Colt as he moved over to the target. "The latch is broken!" he said as he opened the window and holstered his gun.

"Hallelujah!" Hosea declared in a loud whisper. "That's an answer to prayer!"

Stacey looked doubtful. "When did you pray for a broken latch?"

"Well . . . what I meant was . . ."

"Never mind that!" Dehner anxiously whispered. He was looking out at his companions after having crawled through the window. "Get inside!"

Hosea and Stacey complied. The three men were now standing in a large storage area. Stacey's voice was uncharacteristically nervous. "Ah . . . Hosea, do you know if Gail might be, um . . . with a client?"

Hosea hastily shook his head. "If an owlhoot wants to spend more than an hour with one of the girls, he has to take her to a hotel. Beau Rawlins's orders. But listen here. Gail don't—"

Dehner cut him off. "We have to get moving. We don't have much time. One of the other jaspers guarding the town will find the two we tied up soon enough."

Dehner carefully opened the door that led into the saloon proper. The detective immediately remembered Hosea's statement about the occupants of Devil's Due preferring darkness to light. The Fast Dollar seemed dedicated to an eternal night. Two thick doors that fronted the bat wings stood closed. The saloon's four small windows were covered by thick curtains. Smoke from the previous night circled about the room like a vicious snake. No one had bothered to stack the chairs on the tables. Many of the chairs were scattered about the saloon like confused drunks. The air was rancid with the odor of tobacco, booze and urine. Broken bottles lay scattered on the floor.

The kerosene lights were glowing on the large wagon wheel chandelier that hung over the Fast Dollar, but the chandelier didn't seem to provide illumination. Rather, it cast a shimmering yellow stain over everything it touched.

"If Satan has an office, this must be what it looks like," Hosea said. The other two men nodded in agreement.

Dehner gave the preacher an anxious look. "We have to move quickly. You're going to have to wake Gail up if—"

"I will, I will, she's right up the stairs." Hosea led his companions up the stairway.

When they reached the top, Hosea made fast but quiet steps toward the room where he had talked with his Gail on the night Lars Olsen had beat him up. As he opened the door, the three men glanced toward the bed where Gail lay. The girl looked pale and was breathing rapidly, like someone in pain. Her hands clung to the white sheet that covered her as if it were a flag of surrender.

"Wake her up, Hosea. But we haven't got much time." Dehner and Hooper stepped away as Rance closed the door. Hosea Rimstead was alone with the woman he loved.

Chapter Twenty-Three

He walked over to the bed and gently touched her on the shoulder. "Gail, wake up."

"Whaa—Hosea—what are you doin' here?"

"I'm here with Stacey Hooper and Rance Dehner. We're here to take you away from this here—"

"Go away, Hosea, please, go away."

"Look, Gail, Beau Rawlins's days are numbered. You don't—"

"Please, Hosea, leave."

"Look here woman, how many times have I got to explain to you, the Lord wants—"

Gail's voice took on a bitterness that stunned her companion. "You're mighty good at tellin' me what the Lord wants. Did it ever occur to you, Hosea, that what the Lord wants always happens to be exactly what you want?!"

Hosea Rimstead took a step back from the bed, a shocked expression on his face. "You're right . . . I never thought of it that way, but . . . you're right."

Gail looked away. Her eyes fell on two roaches scampering about on the wall to her left. The young woman thought the insects looked like the happiest ones in the room. She turned back to Hosea but couldn't think of anything to say.

Hosea crouched down beside the bed. "Gail, I've made some bad mistakes. But I have a need to preach. This part of Texas is called God forsaken. It's not true. God forsakes no place and no one. I hav'ta tell folks that. It's somethin' I just gotta do. I really think the Lord sent me here when I was headin' for Capstone because of you. I can't do nothin' without you. I love you so much, Gail. Please . . ."

Stacey Hooper lifted his ear off the bedroom door. "It's very quiet in there. At least our prophet is not prophesying. That can get very tedious and is certainly no way to win a lady's heart."

"He's been in there too long," Dehner said. "We need—"

The detective stopped speaking as Hosea and Gail stepped out of the room, hand in hand. Their faces reflected both happiness and determination. Gail was wearing her red saloon girl dress, the only clothing she had handy.

"We're ready," Hosea said. Gail smiled as if echoing Hosea's remark.

"Well!" Stacey declared robustly. "You two certainly do indeed look ready for whatever the future brings."

Rance hoped they had a future. "Let's go!"

They ran down the stairway. When they reached

the bottom, the gambler pointed toward the back door, "This way."

"Stop right there!"

Stacey Hooper froze and then slowly turned around, as did his three companions. "I don't know your name sir, but your face is familiar. We met earlier in the day. As I recall you were stationed behind a boulder with a rather uncouth gentleman. Both of you were firing at me. You were by far the better shot, sir. My compliments."

"Thanks Fancy Pants, the name is Toby Colton." Colton was standing behind the bar holding a shotgun.

Dehner tried to match Stacey's cordial tone; best to keep the gunman talking. Rance pointed in the direction of the closed front double doors. "How did you get inside, Colton?"

"Been here for hours, I was sleeping behind the bar in a bedroll. Didn't want to pay what those rat hole hotels charge and I didn't want to barge in on any of the ladies upstairs."

"I'm the only one who was sleeping upstairs," Gail grasped Hosea's hand as she spoke in a matter of fact manner. "The other girls are all at one of those hotels you call rat holes."

Toby Colton gave Gail a lustful stare. "Too bad you ain't at one of the hotels, girly. Never cared much for killin' women but I've done it before."

Toby began to lift the shotgun. Stacey again spoke in a friendly robust tone. "Our arrival must

167

have awakened you. My friends and I apologize profusely."

"All them pretty words ain't gonna help ya, Fancy Pants." The smile on Colton's face was chilling: the look of a man who was about to, literally, blow his problems away. "When I got woke up I jus' naturally thought about this scatter gun the barkeep always keeps handy. Ya see, Rawlins doesn't know Polly is still alive. I tole him 'bout us gettin' ambushed and the other jaspers gettin' killed. But I also tole him Polly is dead. He patted me on the shoulder, said he would pay me tonight and then headed home. With you folks around he might figger somethin' went wrong and not pay me."

Colton stepped carefully from behind the bar as he pulled back the rabbit eared hammers on the shotgun and approached the threesome. He noticed them trying to spread out. "I want ever one to stay close together. After all, ya don't want to die alone."

Stacey remained cordial, as if he had just lost a friendly game of cards. "Friends, it appears that the game is over and we have lost. Let us take consolation in the fact that we played well." As he eyed his companions, the gambler gave Dehner a short but significant glance.

The detective looked carefully at their captor. Toby Colton had a Colt .44 strapped low at his waist. The revolver was the gunfighter's weapon of choice. He no doubt had a rifle in the boot of his saddle which he could also handle well. But he held the shotgun in a slightly awkward manner. He hadn't used a scattergun that often.

"I have a little confession to make, Toby," Hooper spoke wistfully. A man resigned to his fate. "Last night, I stole some money from the Fast Dollar. Before you dispatch me to my maker, I would like to make restitution." He started to reach inside his coat pocket.

"Freeze, Fancy Pants!" This time, Colton's shout was filled with anxiety. His eyes grew large and were fixed entirely on the gambler. He took another step toward his prisoners. He wanted one shot to do the trick.

Dehner dropped to the ground and rolled toward Toby Colton. He plowed into the man's legs. Colton stumbled and swung the gun upward as he fired. The shot went toward the ceiling, demolishing the wood and glass of the chandelier and raining flaming kerosene onto the tables and chairs below.

Toby Colton regained his balance and reached for his sidearm. Dehner buoyed to his feet and landed a hard punch under Colton's left ear. A new gust of red surged as the fire gained more strength. Colton staggered backwards and fell into the red blaze. Terrifying cries of pain now came from inside the inferno. Stacey Hooper fired two shots into the fire. There was one more horrifying screech, then the voice of Toby Colton was heard no more.

"An act of mercy," Stacey said with uncharacteristic grimness.

Dehner coughed from the smoke. "We've got to get out of here!"

Hosea and Gail were already standing by the door to the storage room. Rance and Stacey quickly joined them but Rance shook his head when Hosea started to open the door. "By now, those other two guards on duty are outside. The front door is locked. They know we will be coming out the back. We'll walk into a hail of bullets."

Gail put a hand to her throat. "So, we burn to death or get gunned down by outlaws!"

The Fast Dollar was engulfed in smoke as the fire continued on its voracious path of destruction. Ashes tinged with red began to rain all around them.

"What are we gonna do?" Hosea yelled.

Dehner gave the young man an intense stare. "Listen carefully, prophet."

Less than a minute later, Hosea rushed into the storage room. Rance crawled behind him, hoping he couldn't be seen through the window. Hosea leaned against the wall beside the door and began to shout. "Oh Lord, take thy servant away to be with you. You have taken my beloved. You have taken the gambler and his friend. Now, I beseech you to take me. Like your servant Jonah, I beg for the comfort of death!"

Dehner was now at the opposite side of the storage room, crouched down, gun drawn. He heard the laughter outside and watched as the door barged open and two men stepped inside carrying their weapons.

One of them continued to laugh as he raised his Smith and Wesson, "I'll gladly oblige ya, Sky Pilot, ya—"

"Drop the guns!" The two gunmen turned to fire and were met with bullets from Rance's Colt. Stacey and Gail entered the storage room. Dehner picked up the two weapons dropped by the gunmen and handed them to Hosea and Gail.

"You may need these. Help me drag these owlhoots outside." They dragged the two outlaws a safe distance from the burning saloon. The crooks were wounded but conscious. From this point, they would have to take care of themselves. Sounds of panic almost overwhelmed the crackling and collapse of buildings as the fire began to rapidly engulf the town.

Another sound joined the chaotic cacophony: pounding hoof beats. "Sounds like a whole bunch of horses is comin' outta the livery," Hosea shouted.

Dehner led the foursome wide of the fire as they ran around to the front of the saloon. Terrified cries of men and women covered Devil's Due as if carried on the dark smoke which was beginning to blanket the area.

Gail's face turned pale with horror as she took in the scene. "One of the hotels is on fire! Those poor people are trapped . . ."

"We can't help 'em now," Hosea said. "Come on, Gail, let's get the horses Stacey, Rance and me got tied up."

The couple ran off toward the northern end of town where the horses were tethered. Dehner reckoned Hosea was trying to get Gail at least partially away from the terrifying spectacle that was Devil's Due.

The fire was advancing southward at a frightening pace and the people who were now stampeding toward the northern end of town were doing nothing to stop it. Rance figured that even if they started to fight the fire now it was too late. The red embers that glowed demonically from the cloud of smoke would soon attack the buildings on the north end of town. Fire was ravaging Devil's Due making it a hell on earth.

Those who weren't perishing in the fire were running toward the livery. Rance and Stacey joined the mob and as they got closer to the building they could see Beau Rawlins mounted on a horse and yelling at the men around him, many of whom were also on horses.

"Let's ride north about a mile from here. We'll regroup there."

Rawlins's orders were met with a confusion of babble. The outlaws seemed uncertain as to whether they should obey orders from the boss of a town that was being destroyed.

Stacey took advantage of the confusion. "Get free of the fire, then head south, men! The Texas Rangers are here! They're the ones that started the blaze."

The ploy worked immediately. One of the outlaws shouted, "Ride west, we'll get past the flames then head for the border!"

A half dozen men rode off while others ran into the livery for a horse. There was one exception. One rider headed north: Rory Kagan.

"You tellin' the truth about the Rangers, Stacey?!" Rawlins shouted angrily.

"Of course, Beau, you know that a gentleman's word is as good as gold."

Rawlins didn't have time to assess the gambler's statement. Dehner jumped onto the saloon owner's sorrel and the two of them tumbled off the horse. Stacey drew a Derringer from his coat and slammed it on Beau's noggin before he could get up.

Hooper smiled down at his handiwork. His smile broadened as Hosea Rimstead and Gail approached on horseback. Gail was riding Dehner's bay. Hosea's one hand was holding the reins of his own horse and his other hand gripped the reins of the gambler's mount which followed behind him.

"Hosea, toss me a rope," Stacey shouted gleefully. "When Beau regains consciousness, he is liable to be a bit restless. We need to take action to calm his nerves."

Using his fingers as a broom, Rance swept red sparks from his shirt while getting back on his feet. He mounted the sorrel as he looked inside the livery. "There are still several horses inside."

"Don't worry, we'll turn 'em loose," Hosea proclaimed. "We won't let God's innocent creatures perish in the fire."

The detective felt a tad embarrassed. His thought had not been on the same path as those of the preacher. "Good idea, Hosea, but first get a horse for Beau Rawlins, then the three of you take Rawlins into Capstone where they'll jail him. Gail can stay on my horse. I'm using Rawlins's sorrel, the horse is fresh and I need to ride him hard. I'm going after Rory Kagan."

Hooper pointed toward the sky which was now rendered invisible by a gray-black cloud. "But, Rance, it's night, tracking will be impossible."

"I know where he's headed." Dehner gave a two fingered salute, then turned his horse and rode off.

Dehner's thoughts had been on capturing Beau Rawlins and Rory Kagan, his mind rejecting those horrors around him that he couldn't control. But as he rode the sorrel out of Devil's Due he could hear the desperate shouts for help morph into horrifying cries of pain: the final and hopeless petitions of the doomed.

Chapter Twenty-Four

Morning was starting to cut the night as Dehner pulled up in front of the Circle T. The days start early on ranches and the detective wasn't surprised to see a handful of men bustling about, probably getting breakfast ready. Lem Donnigan was not helping to prepare a meal. He stood with a Winchester several yards in front of the ranch house. Elijah Tantrall was approaching the ramrod from the side of the house.

The ranch owner quickened his steps as he saw Dehner rein up in front of Donnigan. "Hello Rance, my daughter told me everything!" Elijah stopped beside the foreman, and caught his breath before continuing. "We have guards posted all over; so far, Lem's the only one that's seen any action."

"Wasn't really much action," Donnigan said.

"What exactly happened?" Dehner asked.

"That fool Kagan kid came ridin' up. Said he wanted to talk with Miss Lilly. I said no. He told me he had to see her. I told him to ride off before I killed him."

"Did he act threatening?"

Dehner's question caused the ramrod's face

to crunch as if he was surprised Kagan didn't become violent. "No, he looked upset . . . sorta like he might cry or somethin'. Didn't say nothin' more but he sure spurred his horse and took off fast."

Elijah shook his head. "When I hired ya to help us Rance, I knew something really bad was goin' on but . . . this whole thing is strange, very strange and very ugly."

"I think it is about to get even uglier," Dehner responded. "I'm going after Rory."

Elijah hastily looked upwards. "There's enough light and it'll soon get brighter. If you're careful ya should be able to track him."

"I don't have to track him. Rory Kagan has only one place left to go to . . ."

As he rode toward the Kagan farm, a tension gripped Dehner. He knew Rory Kagan was dangerous but he couldn't decipher exactly how the young man posed a threat. A strong hatred for his father tormented Rory, but he was still deceptive enough to convince Lilly Tantrall that he was a man of good character. On an entirely different level, Rory was clever enough to set up a land grab scheme with Beau Rawlins.

And, most important, Rory Kagan had killed without apparent remorse.

The sun was in the sky as Rance drew close to the farm. He could see a horse tied to a porch rail at the front of the main house. Not wanting to warn of his approach he dismounted before the sorrel's hoof beats could be heard by anyone at the farm and walked the horse to the back of a tool shed about twenty yards to the side of the house.

Tethering the animal there, Dehner approached the house from the side. As he drew nearer he could hear angry shouts. The detective carefully stepped onto the front porch of the house, paused beside a window and listened. He recognized the first voice as belonging to Glenn Kagan.

"Ya never amounted to nothin', boy and ya never will. I'm gonna drive Elijah Tantrall outta this here area for good. After that, bein' President of the Homesteaders Association will really mean somethun' and—"

"You're pathetic!" The second voice was obviously Rory.

"Whatta ya mean?"

"Sodbusters ain't good for nothin' 'cept raisin' food for the ranchers. The cattle business is where the real power is and I'm gonna be the richest rancher around."

The older Kagan responded with a mocking laugh. "Do tell! You ain't never punched a cow in your life!"

"I won't be punchin' cows, I'll hire ranch hands to do all that for me."

Glenn Kagan's laughter became louder. "And jus' how do ya figger on doin' that?"

"I'm gonna marry Lilly Tantrall!"

"Wha—"

"That's right. I've been seein' her behind your back, old man."

"Ya damn fool!"

"We're gonna find out real soon who's the damn fool. I've fooled ever one, even Lilly. She don't know I planned those attacks on the sodbusters. Hell, I even took part in them. That girl worships me and after we're hitched, I'm gonna be the most powerful man around. You and the others in the Homesteaders Association are gonna survive by eating the crumbs from my table . . ."

Rory Kagan's voice was becoming louder and approaching hysteria. Devil's Due was ashes and so was Rory's scheme for a massive land grab. He was cut off from Lilly Tantrall. The young man seemed to be retreating into his own delusions. Listening from outside, Dehner realized the situation was becoming very dangerous.

Glenn Kagan's next words confirmed the detective's fears. "Put away that gun, whatta ya think you're—"

Dehner drew his Colt and quietly entered the house. He was surprised by the attractive, feminine look of the living room he now stood in. The windows were covered by pleasant, frilly looking drapes. In the center of the room was a small fireplace and the mantel above it held a line of pretty dishes. Facing the fireplace was a sofa with a quilt over it displaying designs of flowers. Beside the fireplace was a hall which presumably led to the bedrooms and kitchen.

Glenn Kagan stood in front of the hallway entrance where he marked the end of the room's pleasantness. He stood unshaven and dirty with wide eyes signaling fear and hatred. The older Kagan wasn't armed.

Rory Kagan held a six shooter in his hand. He was positioned a few feet from the front door. He raised his gun pointing it at Rance while flashing glances at his father. "What are you doin' here, Dehner?"

"I've been listening in to what you said, Rory." Dehner pointed his Colt at the younger Kagan. "None of it surprised me. You're going to jail."

Rory continued to shout his words. "You think I won't kill you because you're a detective? Hell, I've already put Sheriff Max Thompson in the ground."

Rance kept his voice low and calm. "I'll bet Max Thompson wasn't facing you with a gun in his hand."

"That don't make no damn difference—"

"Yes it does, Rory. I can kill you and I will. Drop your gun right now, I'm not asking again." Dehner kept his eyes on the young man's gun hand. Rory's trigger finger was an inch from the trigger. Rory Kagan hadn't wanted to kill his father immediately. He had wanted to taunt him first. That desire placed him at a slight disadvantage as Dehner's finger lightly touched the trigger of his Colt. And Rance could place his bullet where it would mean instant death for the young man.

The detective didn't want to kill Rory Kagan. But the kid was pointing a gun at him from only a few feet. There was a tortured expression on Rory's face. Dehner didn't understand the boy well enough to know what was raging inside him or to anticipate his next move. They were in a standoff. Dehner's eyes remained fixed on his adversary's trigger finger. The detective would have to fire at the slightest indication of movement.

A shot blared through the house. Rory dropped his gun as he plunged to the floor. Rance scooped up the gun then looked in the direction of the hallway where the shot had come from.

Judith Kagan walked briskly toward her fallen son and crouched over him. She placed the pistol she had just fired on the floor beside her, and began to caress her boy's face.

Tears loosened from Rory's eyes as he looked up at Judith. "I would have killed him, Mother. I woulda done it, got rid of that snake who beat both of us, honest."

"I know." Judith gently kissed her son on his forehead. "You are a good boy, Rory. I love you very much."

As she stood up, Judith grabbed the pistol she had laid down and fired another bullet into her son. A shock seemed to pierce Rory Kagan's body, which became totally rigid before going limp.

The detective stared at the woman in total confusion. She still held a gun in her hand but Dehner understood instinctively that he was in no danger.

Glenn Kagan's face reflected astonishment as he walked toward his wife. Standing beside her he glanced down at his son's corpse.

"Ya done right, woman." Glenn's body began to tremble as he had to step back to avoid the blood now streaming from what had been Rory Kagan. "That boy was loco. He got what he needed."

Judith gave her husband a hard stare of absolute hatred. "What my son needed was a decent father." She fired two bullets into Glenn Kagan and showed no emotion as her husband hollered in pain and collapsed.

The woman then dropped her gun to the floor. The motion had an odd sense of finality to it, as if she was gesturing an end to her own life.

Dehner holstered his Colt and shoved Rory's pistol away with his foot. He crouched beside Glenn Kagan and felt the neck for a pulse he knew wasn't there. He returned to his feet staring at Judith.

The woman began to answer Dehner's unasked

questions. "My husband was an evil man because he decided he wanted to be evil. He could have fought the liquor. I offered to help him enough times. But he wanted the false pride that comes with drink. He had to be big and powerful. In trying to make himself that way he turned small and evil like a serpent. Worst of all, he corrupted Rory with his evil."

Rance gestured toward Rory's corpse. "But why—"

A tenderness fell over Judith's countenance. "Rory didn't want to be evil. He fought it but his father pushed him into his own private hell. Glenn Kagan made his son a cripple and then mocked him for being one! Rory became determined to be the big, important man his father couldn't be. In the process he became like his father. Maybe Lilly could have saved him but . . . she came into his life too late."

Dehner made confused motions with his hands. "I still don't understand why you had to kill—"

"I heard you talking with my son. I had suspected he killed Max Thompson but hoped it wasn't true. Max was loved and respected by everyone who knew him. Max was a good man. That's what evil does, it destroys innocent people."

Dehner was beginning to understand the woman's motives. "You wanted to save your son from being hanged."

Judith nodded her head. "I heard everything Rory just told his father. And he would have said the same thing at his trial . . . still trying to be the big man. Yes, he killed Max Thompson! Yes, he arranged the attacks on the farmers. He would have confessed to it all, expecting people to admire him. They would have hated him. They would have shouted awful things at my boy as he walked up the scaffold to be hung. I couldn't let him go through all of that! One more terrible humiliation before he died!"

The woman cupped hands over her face. After a few moments, she lowered those hands using them to wipe her cheeks. "I have a favor to ask of you, Mr. Dehner."

"Yes."

"Could you be so kind as to help me bury my husband and my son? After that you can take me into town and turn me in to the sheriff. I will, of course, confess to everything."

"I'll help you with the burying, but I'm not taking you to the sheriff. There's no sense in doing that, Mrs. Kagan."

"But, you're a detective, I've just killed two men, don't you have a duty to arrest me or something?"

"No," Dehner replied. "Rory was pointing a gun at both your husband and myself, threatening to kill us. You didn't break any law by . . . you didn't break any law."

"But my husband wasn't threatening anyone! What I did to him was cold blooded murder!"

Rance smiled wistfully. "Everyone in Capstone knows what kind of man Glenn Kagan was. The sheriff would never arrest you."

Silence followed and Dehner wondered if Judith Kagan understood what he wasn't saying. Women were considered precious in the West and Judith Kagan was a handsome woman to boot. They weren't going to hang her for killing a snake like Glenn Kagan.

The detective buried both of the Kagan men on the farm. He worked alone while, inside the house, Judith meticulously cleaned up the gruesome results of the bullets she had fired.

After Dehner finished, he politely refused Judith's offer of coffee which he was sure she had made only out of a sense of obligation. "I'll be heading back to Capstone, Mrs. Kagan. I could stop at one of your neighbours and ask them to come by. I hate to think of you being here all alone."

"No thank you, Mr. Dehner. I think I'd like to be alone for a while."

As he rode back to town, the detective reflected on the fact that he had encountered many killers and Judith Kagan had to be the most unusual of the bunch. His mind went back to the town hall meeting where the ranchers and the farmers gathered on different sides of the saloon and

Elijah Tantrall had replied to verbal attacks from Glenn Kagan. He had noticed a lot of unattached men, both farmers and ranchers at that meeting. Most of them were almost certainly widowers.

"Judith had better enjoy her solitude while she can," Rance said to the sorrel. "There will be a lot of suitors calling on her soon."

Dehner remembered the lovely living room where the carnage had just taken place. Judith Kagan enjoyed keeping a good home. He had no trouble imagining her getting remarried and living a calm domestic life.

That thought made him uncomfortable and he struggled in his mind to understand why.

Chapter Twenty-Five

Dehner spoke gently to the lady riding on the spring seat next to him. "You look deep in thought, Miss Stevens."

Polly Stevens looked surprised. She gave a light laugh and returned the smile. "Sorry Rance, it's been so long since anyone has called me 'Miss Stevens' I'd plum forgotten my last name. Please, call me Polly."

"You can relax now, Polly," Dehner said as he directed the two horses on the small buckboard. The wagon belonged to Elijah Tantrall. They were travelling from the Tantrall Ranch to Capstone. Both Rance and Polly were dressed in Sunday clothes. "You'll still need to testify against Beau Rawlins but all the people who might have hurt you . . . well . . . they're gone now."

"That's not the only thing that's changed since yesterday when you came by the Tantrall place to tell us Rory and his papa were dead."

"Oh."

"I didn't have the chance to tell you yesterday but the Tantrall's cook and housekeeper Kate is sick, real sick," Polly said. "She's bedridden, probably ain't got more than a few weeks left and she knows it. Elijah talked to me 'bout it last night. He wants me to look after Kate and take over the cooking and housekeeping."

"I'm very sorry about Kate, but it looks like you have a steady job."

"Yep, Rance, and we both know it's better than what I was doing." Polly went silent for a few moments before continuing. "Elijah and his daughter are such wonderful people. I'm eight years older than Lilly but I can learn a lot from that girl."

"Lilly is one smart young lady but she is naïve, maybe she can learn a few things from you."

Polly smirked in a whimsical manner. "Maybe. Lilly's still hurting over Rory, will probably cry for him a few more times. But she'll get over it. Lilly is taking over the book work from her father, won't surprise me if she doesn't take over the ranch in a few years." The woman smirked again, this time mischievously. "After a spell, she'll start noticing the way Lem Donnigan acts around her. Donnigan is one fine man. They'd make a good team."

Dehner stopped the wagon in front of the small church on the northern end of Capstone. Gail was standing in front of the building and waved at the newcomers. Gail was wearing a new white dress. Rance thought it looked a lot better on her than the red outfit she had worn at the saloon.

Rance jumped from the wagon and helped

Polly down. "I was so happy when Rance told me the news," Polly shouted.

"Thank you for coming, it means so much to have you here!" Gail replied.

The two women embraced each other and started to cry. The detective stood by awkwardly until Hosea and Stacey came out of the church.

"We're all set!" Hosea declared. "Paul Stanwick is ready to do the ceremony. He's an old pal of mine. I was comin' to Capstone to see him when I got lost and ended up in Devil's Due. We are the same kind of reverends."

"What do you mean?" Polly asked.

"Paul and me ain't been to college or nothin' like that but we got preacher's licenses from the Methodist Church. We can preach, do weddin's, baptisms, funerals, all that. Paul has been writin' to the mayor of Gopher Creek, Texas. They need someone there to start 'em a church. So, first thing tomorrow morning, that's where Gail and I are headed."

"Gopher Creek," Stacey exclaimed. "The place sounds like a thriving metropolis!"

"Well . . ." Hosea seemed to be fumbling for a reply.

"Don't take offense, Reverend Rimstead," Stacey said. "I'm quite glad you are going to a location I am unlikely to visit very often. You have been a bad influence on me. I have actually been giving serious thought to some of your assertions.

I need to spend more time with my own kind."

Gail gently touched the arms of Stacey and Rance. "Hosea has told me how kind you've been. Thanks for buying us a buckboard and the nice clothes, we are deeply grateful to both of you.

"It was nothing. After all, a wedding is a time of celebration." The gambler waved his arm, taking in the entire group. "After the ceremonies, all of us and Reverend Stanwick will have a sumptuous meal at the hotel's restaurant. I have also reserved a room for our newlyweds at the same hotel."

Stacey's last statement induced a few moments of uneasy silence. During that time, Dehner mused on the con man he had for a friend. Rance had only learned of the wedding a few hours before and had been dispatched by Gail to ride out to the Tantrall ranch, deliver the good news to Polly and bring her in for the ceremony. The gifts of the buckboard, clothes and meal had strictly been Stacey's doing. But it had been a good idea and the detective didn't mind paying for half of Stacey's generosity. In fact, knowing his friend, Dehner was sure he would be swindled into paying more than half.

Hosea broke the momentary silence. "Well come on ever one, we need to get things goin'."

"You three go ahead," Dehner said. "Stacey and I will be right in."

As soon as their companions departed, Stacey

hastily spoke to Dehner. "I knew you wouldn't object to helping a struggling young couple begin a life of Christian service."

"No objections at all," Dehner replied good naturedly. "I just wanted to know the situation with Beau Rawlins."

"My former employer is resting comfortably in jail. The Rangers will be here tomorrow to take him to wherever they are taking him. Following Beau's departure I will be leaving this town for a yet to be determined destination. What about you?"

"After our sumptuous meal, I'll take Polly back to the Tantrall ranch. I'll stay the night there and leave for Dallas early in the morning. There will probably be another assignment waiting for me at the Lowrie Detective Agency."

"I look forward to our next meeting."

"How do you know we'll have another meeting?" Rance asked.

"As I told Hosea, I need to spend more time with my own kind. My own kind tend to be the ones who provide you with those assignments." Stacey laughed at his own joke and was still chuckling as the two men entered the church.

For three days the ruins of Devil's Due burned and smoldered. The flames and smoke gradually disappeared as the town became a grotesque pile of destroyed buildings and burnt flesh.

Books are produced in the United States using U.S.-based materials

Books are printed using a revolutionary new process called THINKtech™ that lowers energy usage by 70% and increases overall quality

Books are durable and flexible because of Smyth-sewing

Paper is sourced using environmentally responsible foresting methods and the paper is acid-free

Center Point Large Print
600 Brooks Road / PO Box 1
Thorndike, ME 04986-0001 USA

(207) 568-3717

US & Canada:
1 800 929-9108
www.centerpointlargeprint.com